Mr. Chen's Sweet and Sour

a novel by

Chuck Harris

Published by BookLocker.com, Inc., St. Petersburg, Florida.

Printed on acid-free paper.

This is a work of fiction. Although based on actual occurrences it is not an entirely factual depiction of them. Many of the characters are real, and events the author has included happened in the places, times and manner he describes. He created others to fill in gaps in the known story and to provide the reader with Morey and Charley's story as he understood it.

BookLocker.com, Inc.
2017

First Edition

To my father, Maurice (Morey) Harris,
for making this story possible

There never lived a better pal

Or brother or a friend,

And we spent the best years of our lives,

With a love that has no end.

Maurice Vann Harris

Chapter 1: Traveling to Charley

Quickening my pace I rushed through the Vanderbilt Square Station's massive steel doors that warm July morning. I was thinking of Charley. It had been months since I'd seen him. My shaggy haired and driven kid brother had left Syracuse for New York hoping to find work as a musician. And he had found it -- getting paying jobs as a banjo player -- and I was anxious to hear and see first-hand what I had only gleaned, reading between the lines of his infrequent letters.

I was looking up at the departure board when I heard a familiar voice.

"Morey," Frances panted, her face flushed from running across the lobby. A few strands of hair clung to her forehead. "I'm glad you're still here."

"My train doesn't leave for a while. What's up, Sis?"

"I made you lunch. Why spend money for that overpriced train food."

"Fabulous. Thanks a million."

"And I added a strudel. To share with Charley."

"Even better."

I found a window seat in the third car on the 11 a.m. train. The spot next to me would remain empty the whole way, giving me a few hours of privacy and a chance to prepare for the weekend. The train lurched then gained momentum, settling onto a rhythmical sway. I lifted my new leather satchel, black with accordion pleats, opened the clasp and removed the lunch Frances had made. Laying the paper bag on the neighboring seat I started searching through it. I took out the strudel. Thoroughly wrapped (where does Frances find all that brown paper?) its fresh baked aroma escaped, reminding me of October apple picking in Genesee Orchards.

I pulled out a few sheets of Charley's compositions I'd plucked from the pile he'd left in the room on Standard Street we'd shared for eight years. "You can have them, Morey," he had said. "When I get to New York I want to start fresh -- no more of that music from the boonies for the big city crowd."

The tune on top was called Hooterville Stomp. I was struck by the attention he had given even to the title's design: not simple, unadorned, script but highly embellished letters. It was as if he wanted to convey not just the words, but their meaning. There were dashes everywhere -- before, after, above and below the title. And, the way he signed it, with his full name: *Composed by Charles Saul Harris*. I wondered why he included his middle name, not just the initial 'S'. After all, he had hated the name 'Saul'. I remembered him as a ten-year old, writing lists of alternate names that began with an S -- Steven, Stanley, Stuart, Scott, Sam -- searching for one more to his liking. As a sixteen year old aspiring songwriter maybe including Saul made sense. Perhaps he had finally grown to like that middle name, or at least come to accept it.

As I studied the rest of the page, it became clear that the two instruments included, violin and piano, were not equally thought out. The violin part that carried the melody was drawn in bold strokes. The piano part, in contrast, was sketchier, as if only there to showcase the violin. I played the piece in my head. While it seemed vaguely familiar, it had an original flair -- fast tempo, clever chord changes, and quick transitions from low to high notes. It would take some fancy fiddling to play this one, I thought. Although I enjoyed creating tunes and had written some in the past, this one was beyond my writing ability.

I spent the rest of the trip studying the other compositions: Salt City Stomp; Bluein in Red; Bassett's Blues; Strings a Hoppin. I played them one by one in my head and was struck by how different they were. Some were written in a quick, almost frenetic tempo that would make even a casual listener take notice. Others were more like ballads; their long lyrical lines would challenge the performer to sustain notes, many of which would sound foreign to a listener attuned to more conventional sounds.

While they were roughly drawn and in need of some serious editing, the raw talent they reflected was striking. Charley was self-taught. Though he had taken a few piano lessons from Mrs. Rogers, our neighbor, he'd never studied violin or taken a composition class. As a fellow musician who had taken many lessons, I was envious. But as an older brother I was proud.

"Next stop, Grand Central," the conductor announced as he moved briskly down the aisle. I packed up the satchel, pulled the overnight bag from above my seat and joined the line leaving the car. We were salmon swimming upstream, struggling up the stairs to the main hall. Unfamiliar sounds hit me before I could even see the massive lobby. The hushed sounds of the Vanderbilt Square Station back home were replaced by the cacophonous noises of Grand Central. My New York City weekend had begun.

The sounds grew louder as I entered the great hall. The din had been anticipated, but now I challenged myself to tease out its sources. Focusing on the conversations around me I found I could identify most words and phrases, particularly the ones in English and Yiddish. Others eluded me. To my left I heard something that sounded like Chinese. From behind me a phrase in a Slavic tongue. Over all of them the loudspeakers boomed garbled announcements of arriving and departing trains.

Not far from the entrance I noticed a young couple standing still, looking up. They had dropped their bags and were staring at the ceiling, pointing and talking. I looked up and caught my breath. The enormous domed light teal ceiling, resting on two rows of massive columns, was adorned with dozens of gold stars that formed constellations. After a bit I identified Orion and began counting its stars. And to the east I saw the outline of the Big Dipper. How many travelers, I wondered, had walked through this hall and not looked up, missing this unexpected delight.

Then there were the smells. Grand Central was awash in layered, pungent aromas -- part man, part man made. The tang of sweat was in the air, as hundreds gathered here on a warm summer day at the end of their work week. Some were probably waiting for the train that would take them away for a few days of respite from the crush of the city -- to Atlantic City or the Jersey shore. Others were anticipating trains bringing in out-of-town visitors -- parents, aunts, uncles, buddies, and sweethearts.

Walking across the great hall toward the subway station, I passed a string of restaurants tucked into the station's southern wall. The aromas were more enticing -- roasting chickens, freshly baking bread, frying onions and garlic, and the waft of spices, many of which were new to me. I thought of Frances's strudel tucked away in my bag, my mouth watering as I conjured up the taste of its apple and raisin filling nestled in a flaky pastry. Moments later, I took in scents from the flower stalls -- lilacs, lilies, gardenias. And roses, my late mother's favorite.

I descended the stairs to the 42nd Street subway station, dropped coins in the pay slot, and walked to the Uptown platform. The crowd was thinner now. Standing near the back, I again noticed the people around me, particularly the young women. These were not the well-nourished Upstate girls I was used to with their casual cotton outfits and simple hairdos, but slim, high-styled New Yorkers, more carefully put together. Wearing lipstick and rouge they sported high heels and figure-hugging outfits, complemented with hats, gloves and stockings, many with black seams along the back showcasing their shapely legs. While I was eager to see

5

Charley, I was having a grand time just waiting for my train.

Twenty minutes later I was at the rooming house at 46 West 73rd Street. I climbed to the fourth floor and knocked on the door of the apartment Charley shared with two musician pals. I almost didn't recognize the man who answered. The clothing indifferent, shaggy-haired lad who'd left Syracuse was gone. From his neatly trimmed, slick backed hair to his highly polished two-toned shoes, this new Charley was every inch an impeccably groomed young man. And I was struck by the outfit's fine fabric, wondering how he could afford it on an itinerant musician's pay.

But I said nothing.

In truth, he had always been the better looking brother. I had inherited our father's coarse features and mother's small frame. Charley had inherited Dad's height and been blessed with Mom's fine facial features, bright green eyes and jet black hair. His just-stepped-out-of-a–bandbox outfit and my rumpled togs only exaggerated these differences. A casual observer might have pegged him as a salesman or a banker and me as a country boy from Upstate visiting the big city.

"Welcome to my humble abode, brother," Charley said. "How was your trip?"

"Very nice. Not too crowded," I replied. "I had room to spread out."

From the back of the apartment a tall, thin man emerged.

"This is one of my roommates, Ross Mercer. He plays piano with our group. Ross, this is my big brother, Morey."

We shook hands; his grip was firm and his hands large. I imagined those long fingers reaching an octave or more on the keyboard.

It was already past 7:00, late for dinner Upstate but early for the City, as we began to plan for dinner. Charley led us to a Chinese restaurant a few blocks from the apartment.

The restaurant's sign read, MR. CHEN'S SWEET AND SOUR. An odd name for an establishment, I thought. Maybe it referred to the proprietor's mood swings.

The restaurant's narrow front was misleading; once we entered I realized that it had a long, thin footprint, like a 12B shoe. The hostess greeted us, handed out menus, and ushered us to a table near the back.

A few minutes later a slim, well dressed, middle-aged Chinese man glided up to our table, greeting Charley warmly:

"Good evening, Mr. Harris. How is music business?"

"Going great, Mr. Chen. You remember my friend, Ross. And this is my brother, Morey. He's in for the weekend from Upstate."

"Special occasion, then," he responded. "Not order from menu; I bring you best dishes." I took it that Mr. Chen was in one of his "sweet" moods.

I looked around and noticed a large number of Asian diners, reminding me of our mother's advice about picking restaurants. "Listen to the customers," she would say: "They should be speaking Sicilian in an Italian restaurant, Yiddish in a delicatessen, and an Oriental tongue in a Chinese restaurant. And never eat in hotels; they can serve lousy food and still survive."

Soon, Charley's other roommate, Lou Chambers, appeared and Charley introduced us. He was shorter than Ross, but blessed with a leading man's looks. He had just finished an audition as a trumpeter for the Biltmore Hotel Orchestra.

We began talking about music, the interest we all shared. As Charley and Ross talked, I realized that they had worked on quite a number of jobs together in Manhattan, other boroughs and even on Long Island. Charley had mentioned only a handful of them to me since leaving Syracuse; now I wondered what other parts of his life he hadn't shared.

They traded stories of their gigs and assessed the musical abilities (or lack thereof) of bandmates. They were serious about their work -- cared about their performance, the venues, and the audiences. I had never heard of most of the players and song titles they bandied about. As their conversation became more intense, Lou and I were swept to the side. I considered starting a separate conversation with Lou. But then, a petite, Madonna-faced waitress brought steaming bowls of soup to our table. Ross and Charley took little notice.

I concentrated on the first course, wonton soup, one of the restaurant's signature dishes. I had ordered it many times at Syracuse's Sampan Café on Clinton Street, but this version was a revelation. The stock was rich and full bodied, the wontons were plumper and seemed homemade, and there were tiny shrimp floating in the broth. I took my first spoonful and was hooked, thinking that I needed to return to this restaurant, sooner rather than later.

Charley and Ross began to focus on their meal, giving Lou, who had only recently moved to the city, a chance to talk. He shared a story about a gig in Chicago he had played that was reviewed the next day in the Tribune. Laughing, he said the critic had written: "Upon leaving the hall, it was a relief to hear the clanging of street car bells, the rattle of elevated trains, and the blowing of automobile horns after hearing this orchestra play their abominable jazz."

The conversation moved on to our social lives. Lou was determined to go on about a girl he had recently started dating. He described Annie as the most beautiful creature he had encountered since coming to New York. She was a band singer whom he had met on a job and begun pursuing the same night. I gathered that they were now an item, spending every available minute together. Charley and I shared some eye-rolling moments, but were too polite to interrupt his monologue.

Later I learned that "Annie" was Annette Hanshaw and, when I met her in person, I realized that he hadn't exaggerated. Not conventionally pretty, she was a tall, green-eyed, auburn haired young woman with an aristocratic air. After they broke up she had a rather successful run as a band singer. Her relaxed, soulful singing style complemented the larger bands she worked with. She recorded with both Pathe and Columbia, earning residuals that went on for years, even after she married and left the business.

Mr. Chen reappeared and brought out the remaining courses, announcing each with the kind of flourish a proud father might use to introduce his offspring: stir fried chicken; General Tso's pork; and whole fish with garlic sauce.

When the bill appeared, I grabbed for it immediately. After all, I reasoned, I was about to have two nights of free lodging, and I was flush from a monthly bonus from the Hotel Syracuse. Waiting for my change, I broke open my fortune cookie. It read: "Unexpected events await you."

No one objected to my generosity nor did any of my companions seem surprised by it. Returning to the apartment, I unwrapped our sister Frances's homemade strudel, hoping that someone might have enough of an appetite left to try some. Placing it on a plate I noticed an envelope underneath the pastry with Charley's name on it. Handing it to Charley I recognized Frances's handwriting. He accepted it without a comment and slipped it into his breast pocket.

Chapter 2: Concerto in F

The morning sun lit up the front room, waking me before the others. I was still full from last night's meal. That old adage about Chinese food clearly didn't apply to Mr. Chen's offerings. I got up from the couch and began to explore the apartment. The place was neater than I would have predicted, considering that Charley had rarely straightened up on his side of the room we shared as boys. Three bookcases lined one wall, filled with volumes on composition, music history, contemporary plays, and novels. Sheet music was everywhere -- on a side table, on a corner of the dining room table and, oddly, underneath a cactus plant on the window sill. I picked up a few and was struck by their variety: jazz scores; a classic saxophone solo; the complete score to the Marriage of Figaro; a Dixieland jazz tune that I had never heard of. I wondered which items belonged to whom and, in particular, which were Charley's.

A toilet flushed, faucets were turned on and off, and the roommates began to appear, first Lou, then Ron, and finally Charley.

"Did you sleep o.k.?" Charley asked, entering the room.

"Fine. Do you have plans for today?"

"Yup. First, we'll go for breakfast at Rubin's. I have a rehearsal uptown for a Sunday gig. So, you have the afternoon free. And then I have a surprise for tonight."

"Will I like it?"

"Oh yes," he said emphatically. "But that's all I'll reveal."

I was intrigued and sensed it had something to do with music.

Since Lou had plans to spend the day with Annie, Charley, Ross and I headed off to the deli. Like most red-blooded young men, we found our appetites, once again, voracious. We scarped down breakfasts of bagels, lox, eggs, finishing it all off with Danish pastries.

"In between jobs, I'm doing a bit of composing," Charley remarked, drinking his second cup of coffee.

"Can I see some of it?" I asked.

"Not yet, Morey. Let's save it for the next visit," he answered. "It needs editing and the accompaniment need fleshing out."

Ross spoke up. "It's quite original; you could call it a 'new sound' Charley's creating. He's even getting some feelers from publishers."

"Let's not get carried away, Ross," Charley said. "It's too early in the game."

I was taken aback. Why would Ross already know about what Charley was working on, have reviewed enough to label it 'original', be aware of publishing possibilities, and yet I knew nothing about it? And why couldn't I look at it?

After breakfast I played tourist, walking around Central Park and checking out a couple of west side music stores. I met Charley back at the apartment at the appointed hour; we dressed for the evening and grabbed a quick dinner at a nearby café.

"So, brother, where are we going?" I asked.

"I'll give you a hint," he replied. "Levisohn Stadium."

Although I had never been to the complex, I knew it was a massive arena capable of housing thousands. Whatever event we were going to must be something special. We took the BMT subway line to 136th Street, crossed Amsterdam Avenue, and melded into a teeming crowd of well-dressed concert goers.

"Follow me," Charley directed as we threaded our way toward a side door.

"Charley Harris. Two tickets. Guests of Ferde Grofe."

I knew the name; Grofe was Paul Whiteman's pianist and orchestrator. And Whiteman was the conductor who discovered George Gershwin. How on earth does Charley know Grofe, and why did he invite him to this event?

We were seated in the third row of the orchestra section. Looking over the program my pulse began to race. We were going to hear George Gershwin play two of his compositions, Rhapsody in Blue and Concerto in F, with the New York Philharmonic. According to the program Gershwin had just finished the latter piece and was performing it for the first time. He appeared onstage, a thin man with coal black hair. He bowed, sat at the Steinway, and started to play the Concerto. The piece had a formal construction: Allegro, Adagio, and

Allegro Agitato, but the sound was anything but formal. In the piano and trumpet solos I heard echoes of New Orleans and Tin Pan Alley music. And the final movement was pure ragtime. Somehow, it all worked together, reminding me of the other genres, but reworked into something original. I was transfixed.

Rhapsody in Blue came next. While I was familiar with this piece from recordings, hearing it live was a revelation. We were sitting where I could watch Gershwin's mastery of the keyboard. The piece was a simpler composition than the Concerto, but no less lyrical or original. Most of the audience, including me, gave the performers a standing ovation. Charley remained seated.

"Wasn't that great?" I asked him as we exited the stadium.

"Yes and no."

"What do you mean?"

"Well. Gershwin is a genius. The compositions were fantastic, and he played them beautifully. But the Philharmonic. Well, they weren't up to the task."

He went on, walking me through the Concerto, identifying places where instruments sounded off. He seemed to know the names of many of the musicians in the orchestra, even mentioning others not in the Philharmonic, whom he thought would have done a better job with the piece.

Nearing the exit, we encountered an older man who looked vaguely familiar. "Hi, Charley. Did you like the concert?"

"Yes, Mr. Grofe. Especially the Concerto," Charley responded. "And thanks for giving us the tickets."

"Happy to do it. And keep with up your writing. It shows promise."

****

I woke early the next morning and bid my good-byes. I was scheduled to work at the Hotel Syracuse that night, so I was catching the 9:30 train. Retracing my steps from Friday's arrival, I saw that many of the shops had not yet opened, and the station's noises were more muted. Boarding the train I found a window seat and settled in, opening the just-purchased Sunday Times. If I put all the Syracuse papers together, I thought, they would still be thinner than this monster.

I scanned the front page. Babe Ruth had been suspended and fined $5,000 for his frequent absences from batting practice. Professional baseball was not my forte, but the fine and suspensions seemed a bit harsh.

Turning to the Entertainment section I began reading the review of the Gershwin concert. Brooks Atkinson wrote: "Gershwin introduced his new Concerto last night, providing further evidence of the talent of this virtuoso musician. His ability to combine classical structure with contemporary sound is breathtaking. Unfortunately, the New York Philharmonic was not up to the task. The string section among others could barely keep up with the soloist, making this reviewer wish that Gershwin alone had occupied the stage."

Charley could have written that review, I thought. Maybe he has a future as a music critic. I folded up the paper and settled back in my seat. My eyes got heavy.

Smoke. I awake choking, seeing nothing in front of me. Then Frances's voice. Her arms surround me. "Put this over your nose and keep your mouth closed," she says, handing me a wet cloth. She leads me out of the bedroom, down the hallway, through the kitchen, and out the back door. Outside. Fresh air. I hear wheezing and realize it is coming from my chest. Now coughing, I can barely catch my breath.

"Where's Charley?" I scream. "Still in our room?"

"No, over there, with Mom. The medics are working on him."

Now able to navigate, I go over to where Frances has pointed. Mom jumps up and hugs me, squeezing me so hard that my wheezing starts up again.

"You're safe. Thank God," she says.

I look down at Charley. Small and frail, a four year old swallowed up by an adult-sized gurney. His skin is grey. A mask covers his face. He is not moving. An attendant works on him, then they wheel him to an ambulance, Mom following. Frances and I get into a police car. Sirens wail. The car drives away, and I look back at the house. Firemen are hosing the front, still on fire. Smoke billows up past the top of the rear window. Neighbors watch. Frozen. Like statues. Their faces lit by the flames.

"Is Charley going to be o.k.?" I plead.

"Let's hope," Frances answers. "Crouse Irving is the best hospital in the city."

I opened my eyes, smelling cigarette smoke wafting toward me from the row behind. A young female voice with a harsh Upstate accent was talking to her seatmate.

"She couldn't have worn that dress any tighter," she said to her seatmate. "And since when does Ruby drink gin?"

"Forget about Ruby. What about that Greg? Very handsome, and he wouldn't stop staring at you."

I needed to move. I started down the aisle to the front of the train, stopping in the washroom to splash cold water on my face. I sat in the dining car with my sandwich, sipped my ice tea and looked out at the passing landscape, wondering why I had dreamt about that event from so long ago. Now Mom was gone, leaving Dad, ever a ghost-like figure, a widower in his forties.

Frances, still in her teens, became our protector as Dad wandered in and out of our lives. It was Frances who made sure that Charley and I had decent meals, clean clothes, and got to school on time. Frances who made sure that the house was clean, the bills paid, that we had Hebrew and piano lessons and finished our homework. And when Dad did show up at the house, smelling of alcohol, it was Frances who put him to bed. Frances, the one who saved my life, then gave me a life.

Joe met me at the station. My sister had married well. He was a man in whom I could find no faults apart from his tin ear. Since all music sounded the same to him, he was indifferent to it. But he had an eagle eye for beauty. And he had pursued Frances, a Janet Gaynor look alike, besting other suitors. The son of the city's most successful jeweler, he was a partner in an accounting firm. They lived in a large, elegantly furnished house on the city's east side, bordering Thornden Park. My sister had a comfortable life; she had hired help, dressed for dinner, and was even on the synagogue board.

"Frances wants to hear about your weekend with Charley," Joe said. "If you come by at 7:00 you'll still have plenty of time to get to the hotel."

That night we ate in the dining room, enjoying Frances's brisket. Usually Mary, the housekeeper, served the meal, and often there was a young single woman from the synagogue seated across from me. But Mary had the weekend off and the single Temple Concord women must have been otherwise occupied. Mimi and Shirley had eaten earlier and were playing in their room, so there were just the three of us. I was enjoying the informality, as I shared highlights of the weekend, leaving out my concerns about Charley.

During dessert I asked Frances about the envelope she'd put inside the strudel wrapping.

"Help me clean up in the kitchen, and I'll explain it all."

Chapter 3: Midnight Raid

I was a few minutes late for my night shift at the Hotel Syracuse. The hotel had opened a few years earlier with much fanfare. Jackie Coogan was there for the grand opening in 1925 and, just two month ago, Charles Lindberg was a guest during his post New York-to-Paris solo flight tour. It was the largest hotel Upstate, boasting nearly six-hundred rooms. The public spaces were grander than anything Syracuse had seen before -- thirty foot ceilings, imported chandeliers and marble floors. Carved mahogany fixtures and velvet furniture were everywhere. And there were even some high end retail shops off the lobby.

I had worked there for just over a year; the pay was decent and the schedule flexible. If I was offered a band job, I could work my hours around it. My world was in balance.

I'd gotten wind of the opening from my high school buddy, Ethan Berman, whose father was a part owner. Ethan's dad was a music fan and had heard me play clarinet at a Central High dance he'd chaperoned a decade ago. "You've got a really sweet sound, Morey," he'd remarked. "I hope you'll keep up playing after you graduate." It was just what a seventeen year old needed to hear, particularly since our dad was indifferent to his own sons' musical pursuits.

Along the way, I took violin lessons from Myron Levee, generally acknowledged as the city's top teacher. I'd hoped that becoming adept at two very different instruments would boost my chances for work.

Frances and Charley both supported the new venture; Charley by composing exercises I could practice for my fingering and bowing, and Frances by subsidizing my lessons. Over time I became a decent violinist and recently Mr. Berman had helped me secure some gigs at his hotel where I played for weddings and a few bar-mitzvahs.

I was assigned to the hotel's front desk, anticipating a sleepy, uneventful Sunday evening, one that would give me another chance to reflect on my visit with Charley. It was not to be. Around 11:30 two City police officers approached my desk and asked for the room number of Charles Kress. I wondered why Kress, a Syracusan, would be staying at the hotel.

Then the officers headed for the elevators, and I knew something was afoot. Kress was a well-known federal agent; some even called him the upstate "Elliot Ness" for his propensity to stage dramatic raids that garnered positive press for the FBI and himself. While my home town rivaled neither Chicago's bootlegging activity, nor its violent crime, we had our own thriving market in illegal alcohol consumption.

A few minutes later Kress, a large athletic man wearing a dark suit, rushed out of the hotel with the officers and got into a black car. I went to the front door and watched as it headed North on Warren and turned East onto Jefferson Street. I hurried back into the lobby; Jameson, the night janitor, who was cleaning the counter, agreed to watch the front desk for me. My heart racing, I headed toward Jefferson Street and spotted the black car parked in the 200 block, directly across from the Wood Building. I had heard a rumor that there was a large speakeasy on the building's third floor. It had to be a raid.

I tucked myself into a doorway, hoping to be hidden. I was able to see both the car and the building's entrance. For a while nothing happened. How still the city is at this hour, I thought. I must be the only one on the street for blocks around. If I were back in New York, there would be much to watch. Couples would be strolling, taxis passing by, and the buildings lit up. My hometown was a study in slow motion, a place where a midnight raid on a speakeasy was what passed for excitement.

Suddenly a gaggle of uniformed officers appeared, led by Police Chief Martin Kavanaugh. He and Kress went in through the front door. I stood and watched, feeling guilty for leaving Jameson behind at the desk. I justified matters by hoping I'd have a juicy story to report when I returned.

Fifteen minutes later a dozen men and two women were escorted from the building and into waiting police cars. I only recognized one man, Aaron Cohen. He was a friend of Frances and Joe's whom I had met some time back at a synagogue service. I wondered what their reaction would be to learn that a pillar of the synagogue had been arrested. They wouldn't find that out from me. A couple of young men appeared, approached Kress, and started a conversation. Bet they're reporters, I thought. And if so, how did they get here on such short notice?

Back at the desk, I recounted the incident to eager ears. Jameson had his own news to report. Shortly after Kress had left, an attractive young woman who had never checked into the hotel came out of the elevator, scurried across the lobby, and went onto the street. Around 2 a.m. Kress returned to the hotel; it may have been my imagination but he appeared to be gloating.

When my shift ended at 6 a.m., I stopped by a newsstand and picked up a copy of the Post. The headline read: MIDNIGHT RAID AT WOOD BUILDING: 14 ARRESTED. It was accompanied by a photo of Kavanaugh and Kress standing shoulder to shoulder in front of the speakeasy's bar. It was all a farce. After all, we had been a "dry" city for nearly a decade already and most of my friends agreed that Prohibition needed to die sooner rather than later.

I thought of my friend Sonny whose family owned the Haberle Brewery. The business had gone bankrupt back in '18 and dozens of men had been laid off. His folks had to sell their house and move to an apartment. The liquor ban had even affected my work, as there were fewer legitimate venues for musicians; most customers enjoyed drinking while listening or dancing to live music. To me, the raid boiled down to an ego trip for Agent Kress. Later I learned that his triumph was short lived when the raid was ruled illegal by a U.S. Commissioner because it was conducted without a warrant. Now that made me smile.

Later that week the phone rang. It was Louie Meyerman, a jovial fellow who led The Music Makers, a well-regarded local band.

"How are you, Morey?" he asked. "I understand you just came back from seeing Charley in New York. And how's the prodigy doing?"

"Very well. He's had a lot of jobs and is busy composing. And we heard Gershwin live at the Levisohn."

"Terrific. I'm not surprised. You Harris boys know your way around music, and Charley his way around the City."

"Nice of you to say, Louie."

"So here's why I'm calling. I have a large wedding reception at the Onondaga Hotel and I need a good fiddle player. Can you help me out?"

"Sure," I said, realizing that I would need to get someone to cover the night shift that Saturday.

"We're having a rehearsal at 7:00 on Wednesday at the Elks Lodge. You can run through the numbers then."

When Saturday arrived I had learned all the numbers including: Sweetheart; Somebody Loves Me; Sittin in a Corner; Swingin Down the Lane; and There's Yes in Your Eyes. By the end of the evening my fingers were worn out and my clothes sweaty, but I had a grand time with the group, and Louie seemed happy with my work. I noticed that when I played with a group of talented musicians like these, time seemed to stand still as I lost myself in the performance. It was pure joy, and I wanted it to become a regular event.

Over the next few months I began to find more work as a musician. I was able to cut down my hours at the hotel and move to a weekday schedule. The new hours left the weekends open for the growing number of orchestra jobs. I was buoyed by the change; now I was working toward something rather than just marking time at the hotel. I could tell that my playing was improving on both instruments, although most of the jobs I was offered called for a violinist.

My expanding job offers were not just in the city proper but in neighboring towns as well: Auburn, Ithaca, Manlius, and Utica. I needed my own car, so I purchased a 1926 Buick Regal for $350 right off the lot. It proved to be a good investment, freeing me from relying on rides from bandmates or borrowing cars from friends to get me to and from jobs.

I wanted to show off my new toy, and my first stop was at Frances's. She inspected the dark blue machine carefully, running her hand over the finish, sitting in the front and back seat, even opening the trunk. She seemed pleased and declared that her brother was now a proper young man, ready to take out prospective young women from her temple in style. While not the reaction I had expected, at least she approved my purchase.

For the next few days I worked on perfecting my road technique. Since I never owned a car before, my driving was rough; the Regal and I were like two out of sync musicians in need of hours of rehearsal before anyone would pay us. I practiced by exploring my city and its outskirts, navigating around the North Side and Onondaga Lake. I even headed out to Sylvan Beach and later to Verona Beach. Soon I had it down. I was like a ten year old boy, tooling around on his first bike, the destination was incidental; it was the feeling of wheels under my feet and the wind on my face that mattered. I couldn't wait to show Charley my new acquisition.

Chapter 4: Enter Lottie

Frances's matchmaking efforts did payoff. Lottie Deutsch was a cousin of a temple friend. She was a few years younger than I and was working as a salesgirl in Addis's, an elegant women's clothing store on South Salina Street. She was a trim, animated young woman with large hazel eyes and black hair. Frances had described her accurately, including the comment, "Morey, you'll like her. She's energetic and funny and can talk to anyone." I liked her immediately; she was a music fan and loved to dance. She had heard me play at the Hotel Onondaga a few weeks earlier and recognized me at once.

Soon we were having Sunday dinners with Frances and Joe and double dating with Lottie's friend Esther and Esther's boyfriend Sydney. All three loved music and came to several of my jobs. The biggest surprise was that, while not a professional, Lottie had a good singing voice and knew a lot of the current tunes. I even persuaded her to sit in on a set at a Utica gig. She did a fine rendering of It Had to Be You, starting out tentatively, but gaining confidence as the tune progressed. The crowd and my bandmates had assumed she was a professional, hardly believing that this was the first time she'd sung in public and with a live band to boot.

Lottie was unlike my previous girlfriends. They had all been hometown girls; the dimensions of their lives defined by three expectations -- finish high school, work for a few years, preferably as a secretary, and then marry with children to follow. All would take place within the confines of the Salt City. Lottie had greater ambitions. She wanted to attend college and become a retail buyer or store manager. Marriage and motherhood could happen, but in due course. And she was not tethered to Syracuse, for to her New York was a beacon, a place of style and fashion. She was already familiar with the garment district after a trip some months earlier with the store buyer. A quick study, her familiarity with the City's geography surpassed mine.

Beyond our shared fascination with New York, Lottie and I had a similar take on how best to practice our faith. Unlike Frances, neither of us had made a practice of attending services at our respective synagogues -- in her case, Beth Shalom and in mine, Temple Concord. Founded in 1850, Concord was a home for the Jewish immigrants from England and Germany, a group with a worldview more secular than religious.

Later on the city's Jews who came from Eastern and Southern Europe founded Beth Shalom, bringing more traditional practices -- conducting services in Hebrew, seating men and women separately, and donning yarmulkes and tallises.

My Orthodox friends referred to Concord's services as "more Christian than Jewish." True, we conducted our services in English with some Hebrew sprinkled in, had an organ and choir, and we did not expect congregants to walk to Saturday services. However, since Frances lived four short blocks from the building, she usually walked, claiming the exercise was good for her. Benjamin Friedman, Concord's charismatic rabbi, was an approachable leader with a wry sense of humor that found its way into his sermons.

More often than I might have liked, Friday nights found the four of us -- Frances, Lottie, Joe and me -- sitting right of center in the temple's fifth row. My sister would have wanted this to be a weekly event, a prospect that appealed to neither Lottie nor me. When we did attend, after the services Frances, with Joe in tow, ushered us around the social hall like two birds she had bagged in a quail hunt, introducing us with: "You remember my brother Morey and his friend, Lottie, Ruth Deutsch's daughter."

One of the service's main delights for me was the music. While the melodies were simple, they had a timeless quality. As I listened, I closed my eyes imaging the melodies being sung in Berlin, Cairo, or London centuries ago. Taking in the sounds of Adon Olum, Modim Shabbat, Adonai Melach was like the red wine we would be served after the service, sweet, familiar, and comforting. I relaxed as the music washed over me.

After a while, the cantor began his solos, just he and the organ. The soothing sounds of the choir were gone, replaced by a single, powerful tenor voice conveying raw emotion. He leaned back, spread his arms and looked skyward, as if singing to the heavens.

First came Shabbat Zachar, then Hadsh Yameno, and finally Mere Haipah. The phrases started and stopped. Then they were repeated, each time with a different intonation. Softly, then full throated, and then reduced to a whisper.

The congregants looked up from their prayer books, caught up in his performance. Familiar songs were now fresh, as if heard for the first time. The rhythmic range and nearly atonal quality of the singing reminded me of parts of the Gershwin concert Charley and I had attended. I wondered if the composer's inspiration wasn't just Negro spirituals, but these Sabbath melodies as well. Then like the third act in a play, the choir and the familiar songs returned and the service ended.

Another delight was gazing at Lottie during the service. The late day's light streaming through the sanctuary's beveled glass windows bathed her in a warm golden glow. Her black hair shimmered and her skin shone like porcelain. She usually wore well-tailored clothes that set off her petite figure, this time it was a pale pink and white striped suit and a pearl necklace and earrings. And she smelled divine. Her favorite perfume was Lanvin's Arpege, a fragrance that reminded me of honeysuckle and peaches. I thought it was charming that her favorite scent was named after a musical term.

Our dates were dictated by our respective work schedules, and neither of us held bankers' hours. Working in retail sales meant that Lottie worked most Saturdays and holidays, but was off on Sundays and

Mondays. I had the late hours in the hotel and the increasingly frequent Friday and Saturday night gigs. We spent nearly all our days off together.

During the warm weather we rented a rowboat at Green Lake State Park. One day, Lottie looked into the water and remarked on its intense blue-green hue. On the spot we decided to rename the place Emerald Lake. "You know, Morey", she said, "Frank Baum lived just down the road when he was writing his book on Oz. I'll bet the color of this water was his inspiration for Emerald City."

The lake was surrounded by dense foliage, providing some privacy. Sitting across from her in the boat, I admired the way the summer frock set off her pale skin and exposed her well-formed shoulders and arms. I noticed dew-like drops of perspiration just above her upper lip. As we kissed I held the small of her back and was transfixed, thinking only of my Lottie. She began to tremble, and I sensed a growing passion in her kisses, and I responded. I wanted the afternoon to never end. I had called Charley after our third date to tell him about Lottie. He listened patiently to my monologue, finally responding, "Yes, she sounds like Frances described her. You're a lucky guy, Morey. I'd like to meet her one of these days."

As sweet as our relationship was it had one sour note which I discovered during one of our midweek dinner dates. We were sitting in a back booth at Caroma's, an Italian restaurant on the city's North Side. We had just polished off our spaghetti carbonara and were waiting for our dessert. The restaurant was all but deserted.

"Lottie, we've been dating for several months, and it's been perfect," I began.

"I agree, Morey, but I sense a serious question is in the wind," she replied. "Am I right?"

"Well, it's about your folks. They live fifteen minutes from here, and I have yet to meet them."

"My mom is happy that I have a nice Jewish boyfriend and would like to meet you. But my dad. He's another story."

"Another story?"

"I'll always be his 'little girl', and he wants 'the best' for me," she replied, rolling her eyes as she said "little girl" and "the best."

"And, I suppose that I don't qualify, being just a part time musician and part time hotel clerk."

"That's some of it," and with obvious reluctance, she continued. "Frankly, he's a lawyer and he thinks that gives him license to judge everyone."

"How so?" I asked wondering what was coming next.

"Believe it or not, it's your family. In his eyes they are Jews in name only and don't seem to practice the faith. My boyfriend should not just be a Jew, but a practicing Orthodox one."

"I see. But you're a twenty-three year-old woman, working full time and sharing an apartment with a roommate. Not a teenager living under his roof."

"Well, he's not happy about my work or my apartment either, although has come to accept them.

But the notion that I am forsaking his synagogue to attend the 'Church of Concord' drives him to distraction."

"That doesn't sound promising," I said.

"I'm working on changing his mind," she said softly, "but it's going to take time."

Dessert arrived, and we ate it silently. I began to wonder how strong a grip Herman Deutsch had on his daughter.

Chapter 5: Tribal Warfare

Lottie's revelation had left my head whirling. How could this be happening? I could have understood her father wanting his daughter to date a man planning a more conventional career, one that fit the traditional model of a prospective Jewish son-in-law—a banker, a physician, an accountant, or even like him, a lawyer. But the thought that differences in how we practiced a shared religion would make me unfit was baffling. It was something out of a fifteenth century folktale in which a boy from the neighboring village pursues the chief's daughter. When the chief discovers this, he has the boy killed to prevent polluting the tribal bloodline. I had been blindsided and had difficulty containing my anger.

I needed to talk to someone. Someone who could help me make sense of this nonsense. Charley was a possibility. But he was now in New York caught up in his career and likely to dismiss the whole affair as silly. He would probably conclude that dating Lottie was a losing proposition and remind me that there were plenty of other eligible women around. That's the last piece of advice I wanted to hear.

I called Frances.

"Sis, I have something I need to discuss. It's important, so I want to talk face-to-face."

"Morey, I'm all ears. Come by for dinner tonight. Joe is working late at the office, and I'd like the company."

Arriving at Frances's I was greeted by the aroma of Mary's stuffed cabbage. It's one of my favorite dishes, but my focus was not on food that night.

"So at dinner last week, Lottie informed me that her father does not approve of me. Guess why?"

"I can't imagine. You're not perfect, but in my eyes, pretty close."

"At first I thought it was because I'm a musician, that's a reservation I can understand. But it's not that. We Harrises don't seem to be acceptable to the Deutsches because we're not religious enough. As I get it, Mr. Deutsch wants his only daughter to date a yarmulke wearing, daily praying, kosher food eating, orthodox Jew. Does that sound like me?"

"Hardly. Have you thought about converting? Moses Braude, at Beth Israel, is looking for new members."

"Very funny," I said.

"Now that I think about it, maybe it's not that surprising."

"Why not?"

"You know, Morey, as bad as the prejudice is against our people, and heaven know it's rampant, we have our own version."

"Our own version?"

"We were always a family of outsiders, even in our community. Dad never earned much, and there were times when we struggled to pay the rent. Religion was important to Mom, and after she died I made sure that you and Charley got a Jewish education. Concord offered scholarships, so that's where you went. Under different circumstances you could have been raised Orthodox."

"But Frances, look what you and Joe have now. Haven't you (I really meant 'we') moved up a few rungs?"

"I suppose, but some people need to feel superior, and Herman Deutsch appears to be one of them."

"So it's not just that we are not Orthodox?"

"What do you think, Morey? It's a ruse; we will always be 'those poor Harrises' in the eyes of the local Jewish elite. I only hope that Lottie can break away from that family mold."

A few weeks later the four of us, Frances, Joe, Lottie and I, were sitting in our usual spot for a Friday night service. Lottie and I were still dating, but had avoided broaching the subject of her father's disapproval. Looking over the program I read the title of the sermon, "Tribal Warfare." The title intrigued me. Maybe it had something to do with the Onondaga or Mohawk Indians, tribes that roamed the county before the 'White Man's' invasion. I couldn't have been farther off the mark.

"We are engaged in a new war," Rabbi Friedman began, his powerful voice filling the sanctuary. His was a voice, confident and direct, a voice that made everyone, adult and child alike listen. Some younger members of the congregation, even thought that it was the voice of God himself. "One that is unique to our country and time. It is between Jew and Jew, each side believing that it has the corner on how to practice our faith and unwilling to recognize the legitimacy of how his brother practices his. It is a new breed of internecine warfare that is taking place right here in Upstate New York. Its consequences are dire for every one of us."

He went on to remind the congregation that the Reform movement was widely accepted in Germany where it had originated. When transported to the States, Reform Jews were now a minority, numerically and socially.

Their counterparts from Eastern and Southern Europe embraced Orthodox or Conservative practice as the way to live the faith. It was as if he were talking directly to Lottie and me; we looked at each other, nodded, and wondered what he would say next.

"I have been concerned about this festering intolerance among our own people, a people that have survived centuries of attempts by non-Jews to snuff us out. While as a people we have never had empires or large armies to defend ourselves, we have survived because of our faith. Now we are engaged in a battle of how best to practice that faith, and I believe that there is no one way. In God's eyes we're all Jews. To that end, early this year I established an intra-faith committee composed of a dozen of my fellow rabbis. Our purpose is to begin a dialogue exploring what we have in common, rather than what separates us. Beginning this fall, we will be offering a series of open forums seeking to build bridges between the Orthodox, Conservative and Reform congregations in our area. I hope that you will join me in supporting this important endeavor. Good Shabbas."

The Rabbi and my sister opened my eyes to a new reality. I'd thought that we Jews were a tight knit group, marked by mutual respect and support. There were around 12,000 of us in a city of 150,000. The number seemed even larger to me; I saw fellow Jews everywhere I looked: the Lewises ran the neighborhood grocery, the Besdins and Bermans the local bakeries, and the neighborhood drug store and cleaners were owned by Jewish families. Many of the local bands, Wally's Rhythm Makers, Pep Barnard's Orchestra, The Ipana Troubadours, were composed mainly of Jewish musicians. And most of the guys I palled around with were Jewish, as were the girls I dated beginning in high school. Our homes, schools, community centers and synagogues were concentrated on the east end of the city. While some families were wealthy, others poor, these differences did not seem to matter.

Later, as I started playing jobs, I stepped out of my East Side bubble and befriended Irish, Italian and German musicians from the North and South Sides. Soon I discovered that just as I was ignorant about the intricacies of life among the "others", they knew very little about my culture. In their eyes, their Jewish neighbors were still living in another world. Some wondered why I never wore a kippah on my head, or dressed as they did, or wasn't planning to be a banker or shop owner. Or why I liked jazz. Others thought it strange that I was hanging out with them on a Saturday instead of sitting in a synagogue, praying. So my understanding of prejudice had centered on how Christians saw us. Now I needed to think about how we saw ourselves.

Chapter 6: Three's a Crowd

Lottie and I had been dating for six months. To mark the anniversary I decided to change things up a bit. In place of a Sunday dinner at Caroma's, we drove south toward Ithaca to try out a new Chinese restaurant, one that several friends had recommended. They described it as "more authentic that anything Syracuse offers." It was a clear October day, and my Regal had just been tuned up. It swallowed up the Onondaga hills like a thoroughbred. The smooth hum of the engine and the solid feel of the tires on the road gave me a comfort I had missed in the stop and go of city driving. I cracked the windows. The crisp cool air bathed our faces, washing away the cares of the workweek.

Lottie looked so appealing that I had trouble keeping my eyes on the road. Fall had always been my favorite season; the sunsets were spectacular, the air smelled fresh, and the landscape took on the red, yellow and gold pallet that I favored. As if sensing my reverie, Lottie began musing on fall and women's clothes.

"You know, Morey, this is the time of year that women's clothes get interesting."

"How's that?"

"The spring and summer offerings are o.k., but pale in comparison to the fall and winter ones. The material gets more interesting—thin cottons, silks and laces give way to wools, heavier cottons, and gabardines. Now, a woman can layer clothes, add a jacket, a scarf, or a vest. Hats begin to make more sense and a coat can set off an outfit. Summer and spring fabrics are more limiting and flimsier, prone to wrinkling. Winter material. Well, it wears like iron."

I had never thought about material that way, but it was Lottie's passion. For me clothing is a functional item, something to keep out the elements and provide places to hold my wallet and keys. Like most men I can't tell silk from sharkskin or cotton from cashmere.

My standard outfit consisted of dark pants, black, blue or brown, a white shirt and leather shoes and belt. On occasion I might add a bit of color and pattern in a tie, but on the whole I am indifferent to even this accessory. In a quest to improve my attire, Lottie had taken me to Brooks Brothers one Saturday. Soon, I was wearing tailored pants, colorful ties and socks. My co-workers at the hotel began to notice, and I even had a guest ask where he could find the blue and grey striped tie Lottie had picked out.

As indifferent as I had been to men's clothing, I usually notice what women wear, especially if they are attractive. I dislike drab tones on women, preferring to see them in colorful patterns -- stripes, checks, and florals. On Lottie, pinks, yellows and blues look striking. I guess she was just born with good taste.

The Peking House proved to be worth the drive. The dining room was elaborately decorated in rich reds and blacks with comfortable seating and gas lighting that shed a golden glow -- a smaller version of Mr. Chen's. Even the menu was similar, a heavy oversized document with an ornate cover. The dishes were grouped by main ingredient: Pork, Beef, Fish and Chicken. Their names were in Chinese script with English translations below. Each was labeled: "mild", "hot" or "very hot".

I suggested we might order some of the same dishes Charley, his friends and I had had in New York, thinking it would be fun to compare the restaurants. Lottie readily agreed. As each one appeared I conjured up an image of Mr. Chen's version. The Peking House dishes were similar: generous portions and nicely plated. General Tso's chicken was a standout and could have come right out of Mr. Chen's kitchen. We could identify each ingredient -- ginger, garlic, scallions and vinegar. We agreed that it was leagues above the Sampan Café's muddled version. Other dishes didn't fare as well, but for an Upstate establishment the food was a revelation.

"Morey," Lottie began, "speaking of Mr. Chen's, tell me more about that visit to Charley."

"Well, you already know the high points, great dinner, meeting his new friends, and the Gershwin concert. But there were some odd notes too."

"Like what?"

"Oh, I don't know. I went to see Charley, but it was as if I had encountered someone else."

"What do you mean?"

"Well, he looked different, more polished, more professional, and more distant than the brother I'd remembered. And there was this mystery; there were things about his life in New York he had never bothered to mention. Things I found out by accident."

Suddenly, I had a thought. "Charley said he would like to meet you. How does a trip to New York sound?"

"Terrific. I'm scheduled to go on a buying trip to the City with my boss in three weeks. Could we arrange to meet him then?"

*****

Three weeks later, Lottie and I were in New York. Lottie was on a three-day buying trip with her manager at Addis's. They were visiting wholesalers and ordering stock for the store's spring line. I was staying with Charley, having taken him up on his open-ended invitation to "Visit me anytime." Lottie had been working long days in the City, and I had not seen her all week. She stayed an extra night to give us time together. And to meet Charley. I picked her up at 6:00 at her hotel, and we planned to ride the subway back to Charley's neighborhood. At last, two of the most important people in my world were about to meet, and I was anxious.

It's curious how people who have been dating a while fall into routines, often unaware that they have. Lottie and I were a case in point. We had become Friday night temple goers and had lost track of the number of times we went to Green Lake, taking out a rowboat or walking the trail that encircled it. Then there's our dinner choices; they too were limited. Most Sundays found us at Caroma's or The Villa, two so-so but conveniently located Italian restaurants. Our Peking

House visit was an aberration, part of my transparent attempt to recreate the meal I had had at Mr. Chen's.

I waited for her in the lobby. I heard the familiar sound of her heels, that quick determined cadence, approaching from behind. I turned around, and my eyes widened. Lottie looked stunning. She was wearing a figure-hugging, calf length red dress with a shiny black belt that matched her shoes. Her shoulder length hair had been done in a new style, fuller with more waves than usual. Even her eyes seemed brighter, the hazel color looking green in the lobby's warm light. Several other men noticed her. They smiled. She returned their smiles, appearing to enjoy the attention. We embraced and headed for the subway.

"You look wonderful," I said. "I like you in red."

"Well, I want to make a good impression on Charley."

"I'm sure you will. He'll love you as much as I do," I answered as we walked to the nearby Broadway Line stop. Charley had an afternoon rehearsal, so I didn't want to ask him to travel uptown. "You know, Lottie, here we are traveling all the way to 10th Avenue to eat at the Chinese restaurant I have already been to, when there are dozens of other spots in Charley's neighborhood."

"But I thought the whole idea was for me to meet Charley. Isn't that his favorite neighborhood restaurant?"

We heard the shower running when we entered Charley's apartment. I called through the bathroom door, "We're here, brother."

"I'll be dressed in ten minutes," he answered. "Made a reservation at Mr. Chen's. Table in the back, so we can talk."

Lottie busied herself by looking through the bookshelves in the living room. I noticed that she pulled out some of the same volumes I had during my first visit, opening several.

"I'd have guessed they'd be about American music or jazz. These cover opera, classical music and there's even one on Klezmer songs. Which ones are Charley's?"

"Most of them, Lou and Ross are not big readers. Charley is interested in all kinds of music, contemporary, classical, American, European. He even likes folk music."

She sat on the couch and began reading a volume on Verdi operas, noting that she had seen Aida three times, but that La Boheme was her favorite, calling it "a sad, romantic story told through great music."

Charley appeared. He had donned another fashionable, perfectly tailored outfit, and his two-toned wingtip shoes were a standout. Frances must have subsidized that purchase, I thought. I introduced him to Lottie.

My brother's reaction echoed that of the men in the hotel lobby. His eyes opened wider, and I thought I heard him exhale.

"I'm happy to finally meet you." Turning to me he added, "Morey, you said she was pretty, but this...."

Lottie looked away, a bit embarrassed. A second later I caught a glimpse of her eying Charley, liking what she saw. Observing the two of them, I thought what a striking couple they would make; they shared the same slim frames, fine features, and nearly identical coloring. Two department store mannequins come to life.

Mr. Chen greeted us as we entered, "Charley, you brought brother back. And who this lovely woman?"

"This is Morey's girlfriend, Lottie. Lottie this is Mr. Chen, a good friend of mine."

"I'm happy to be here. Morey has told me that you have the best food in the City," Lottie said, smiling.

"Hope we don't disappoint," Mr. Chen replied, showing us to the same table where we had sat during my last visit.

After we ordered, Charley asked Lottie about her week. "Morey tells me that you were here scouting out merchandise for the store."

"Yes, this is only my second buying trip; before I came here I had no idea that the garment district was so large. It takes up a whole section of the lower east side. So much merchandise is made in this town. I spent most of my days trailing Helen, our buyer. Together we decided what would and wouldn't work on our floor. We had to pass on a lot of interesting, well made clothes."

"What did you reject?" I asked.

"Well, what Helen or I might like, would be on target for New York, but not for our customers, especially the older ones. They have more traditional tastes."

"Right, that old Syracuse/New York divide. I know it well," Charley exclaimed. "Take music, for instance. What's hot now in Syracuse, was popular here four or five years ago. New York is where the trends start. Syracuse is where they go to die."

"My brother the cynic," I laughed.

Smiling, Lottie chimed in, "But\ in fashion some trends turn into classics, like padded shoulders or tailored skirts. Women will continue to buy them year after year because they look good on everyone."

"But you know there are some things about Syracuse I miss," Charley said.

"Like what?" I asked.

"Well, when I was working Upstate with Jimmy Long's orchestra and, later, the Moonlight Serenaders, we were just a few guys, around eight -- piano, drums, violin, banjo, sax and horns. The music we played was nothing novel, but the audience could see us up close, and there were plenty of chances for solos."

"And in New York?" I asked.

"Here in the City, it's all about big bands. Unless you go to some of the smaller clubs, most jobs are big productions, fully orchestrated and carefully rehearsed. Each band tries to create a certain sound, and the individual players get lost in it. The music is top notch; I have to be on my toes to keep up. But in some ways it's not as much fun."

My brother was opening up, talking candidly about his life here. I wondered if he would have revealed any of this if Lottie were not sitting with us. She had a disarming effect on people, and I was enjoying hearing it all. Our seating pattern had formed a triangle, allowing me to see both Charley and Lottie. When Lottie or Charley spoke, the other's head nodded in unison. They were like two marionettes. It was almost as if an unseen puppeteer was synchronizing their movements, dancing them in rhythm to a silent ballad. I had hoped that they would get along, but I had not anticipated that they would click. A stranger observing them would assume they were old friends, not two people who had met for the first time that day. Was it my imagination or were they too much in sync? I was at once pleased and uneasy.

A slim Asian man approached our table, Mr. Chen minus twenty years. Charley stood to greet him, "William, how have you been?"

"Excellent," William answered. "I finally worked out the fingering on Page Mr. Satan, your new piece."

"Terrific. Folks, this is Mr. Chen's eldest, William. William, this is my brother Morey and his girlfriend Lottie."

"Hello, William," Lottie and I answered, simultaneously.

"Charley has told me a lot about you, Morey. Aren't you the one who got him started in music?"

"I am," I said, "but now the student has surpassed the teacher."

"Nonsense," Charley said, "you're a talented violinist. I have been working with William for a while, helping him to master the banjo. He's a real jazz fan, and he has a feel for the music and some ability on the instrument."

"My folks bought me a five-string tenor for my birthday, and Charley's been helping me get the hang of it."

"The Chens have an apartment upstairs. We meet there once a week. It's quieter than my place. A much better spot for our lessons."

"How lucky you are, William, to have such an able teacher," Lottie said.

"Thanks," Charley answered, seeming a bit embarrassed by the compliment.

Turning to me, "I'll let you know a good time when you and Lottie can come back to the City and hear me play. We're a very tight group, play with a lot of energy and great rhythm."

"We'd like that," I said.

So Charley now has a young student to work with, I thought. And it's interesting that my brother is not only a regular customer but a friend of the Chens and their son's music teacher. His roots in New York seem to be growing deeper. Any hopes I might have had that Charley would be back in Syracuse one day were fading.

Chapter 7: Tova/Toto

The garbled sound of the announcement confused us, but we managed to find the right track and board the Syracuse bound A35 in time, grabbing two adjoining seats. It was hard to find space overhead for Lottie's second bag. Another passenger had set two bags side by side. I stacked them, squeezing Lottie's just-purchased red leather overnighter beside them and sat down.

Shrugging her shoulders Lottie said, "There were some must-buy outfits I spotted at the factories. Great deals. I needed a new suitcase. Music is Charley's addiction, clothes are mine. Aren't we a pair?"

"Yes, and maybe one day I'll find my addiction," I said.

"This was a good trip. I wish I could have stayed longer and had a chance to hear Charley perform. Your brother is a charmer who is turning into a real New Yorker."

"I am glad that you two hit it off."

"So am I. Were you and Charley close growing up?"

"Yes. Even though there is almost five years between us. As a kid, he idolized me. We got into a lot of trouble together. Our folks were not very attentive; Mom was sickly and Dad was rarely around."

'So you were left on your own?"

"Not really. Frances was the real parent. The one that made sure we had regular meals and did our homework on time. She even saved my life when our apartment burned down. Mom had rescued Charley, but Dad was nowhere in sight."

"Amazing. My parents are the attentive type, maybe too attentive."

"Speaking of parents, how is the 'warming them up' regarding our dating coming along?" I asked.

"Rather well. I have succeeded in wearing them down. Now I think it's time for you to meet my folks."

"Looking forward to it."

I unfolded the day's Times. Lottie took the city news section, and I started in on the front. Later, Lottie pulled out her knitting bag. She was working on a red and grey scarf to go with one of her newly purchased outfits.

*****

Ten days later Lottie and I were standing on the Deutsch's front porch. They lived a couple of blocks from Frances and Joe, Syracuse's version of an upscale Jewish neighborhood. The house was an imposing three story Victorian complete with turrets, a wraparound porch and shingles everywhere. An awfully big house for two people, I thought. But maybe that's what lawyers spend their money on. Fancy downtown offices and palatial homes to mark their success and impress clients.

Lottie knocked and I heard a dog bark.

"That's Tova," she said as her mother opened the door. Lottie and her mom embraced, a peck on each cheek, European style. "Mom, this is Morey. Morey, my mom."

"Welcome, Morey. I'm Ruth Deutsch. Good to meet you."

"And it's nice to meet you as well," I answered noting how much mother and daughter resembled each other.

Tova, a small brown and tan terrier, sniffed the cuff of my left pant leg. Appearing to find nothing of interest, he stopped abruptly. Employing a hopping gait that I took as canine enthusiasm, he followed us into a spacious, formally furnished living room.

A tall, bearded grey haired man wearing a dark suit and a yarmulke stood resting his elbow on a Steinway baby grand. I wondered if it was ever played or was only there for effect. Lottie greeted her father in the same peck-peck manner.

"Herman Deutsch," her father said to me, extending his hand.

I offered mine. "Thanks for inviting me to dinner. I look forward to getting to know both you and Mrs. Deutsch."

"Tova, that's an interesting name for a dog," I commented. "How did you come up with it?"

Lottie's mother explained, "Well, his formal name is 'Kelev Tova'. That's 'good dog' in Hebrew. It's a mouthful; we needed a nickname. 'Kelly' was a possibility, but we thought it sounded Irish. After all, we have very little in common with that rough Tipperary Hill crowd up on the North Side."

I wonder how my bandmate, Jerry Murphy, would react to that remark, I thought, trying to show no reaction.

She continued. "So we went with 'Tova'. Suits him much better. After all, he's a Jewish dog. He even eats kosher food." I caught a half smile on her face and thought, I see where Lottie's humor comes from.

Tova, curled up at Lottie's feet, perked up his ears each time his name was mentioned.

"Sounds a lot like 'Toto' from the Wizard of Oz," I remarked, turning toward Lottie.

"You noticed," she answered.

"Dinner will be ready soon," Mrs. Deutsch announced, walking toward the kitchen.

"Would you like to see my old room?" Lottie asked. "It's right upstairs."

Her bedroom was spacious, far larger than the one Charley and I had shared growing up. It was the room of a young girl, flowered patterns everywhere, on the bedspread, pillows, drapes and chairs. A dozen dolls were piled on the bed. They were all facing in the same direction, an audience waiting silently for a performance to start. Framed sketches of women in dresses were hung above a desk.

"Did you do those?" I asked, pointing to the sketches.

"Ages ago, when I was thinking about becoming a designer."

"Very nice," I commented.

I began examining the contents of a large bookcase to the left of the desk. It was a miniature version of a K to 12 library. The books ranged from those a parent might read to a one-year old, to beginning reader books, to teen novels. They were arranged in order, from pre-reader to advanced reader. Seventeen years of reading on four shelves.

"I encouraged Mom to pack this all up and make this a guest room," Lottie said, "but she has yet to do it. It looks exactly like the day I moved out."

Pointing to the top of the bookcase she said, "This is my Frank Baum collection, eight of the fourteen volumes of his Wizard of Oz series. Mom was a friend of Frank Junior, everyone called him 'Bunny', and he had his dad sign several of them for her. Now they're mine."

She picked up the first volume, "The Wizard of Oz", showed me the author's signature and leafed through the first two chapters, remarking on the quality of the illustrations. The colors were intense, and the characters' costumes and expressions were striking.

The dinner conversation went surprisingly well. I had expected a barrage of questions about my career plans, knowledge of Hebrew, and family history. But there were only questions about Charley and an apparent interest in how his career was progressing. Lottie brightened visibly when describing the New York City trip. Mrs. Deutsch raised the possibility that she might lose her daughter to the 'Big City' someday. Mr. Deutsch winced at the suggestion, but said nothing. My stomach tightened at the thought.

After dinner we moved to the living room. Mr. Deutsch sat down at the baby grand and began warming up his fingers, playing a few arpeggios. He seemed at home at the keyboard, even removing his jacket and tie.

"Come, Lottie," he said, "let's entertain Mom and Morey."

"Alright, Dad. If you insist," Lottie replied, taking a seat next to him on the bench.

Mr. Deutsch began a peppy intro, then Lottie sang:

"Oyfn pripetshik, brent a fayerl
Un in shtub iz heys,
Un der rebe lernt kleyne kinderlekh,
Dem alef-beys."

It was a traditional Yiddish song about a home with a fire burning in the hearth. A rabbi is teaching the alphabet to the young children gathered around him. A simple tune played in staccato tempo with Lottie's sweet voice carrying the melody.

The song ended. "Let's hear Adir Hu," Mrs. Deutsch said. Lottie's father began playing, his head nodding with the tempo.

"Adir hu, adir hu
Yivneh veito b'karov
Bim'heirah, bim'heirah, b'yameinu b'karov
Ei-l b'neigh! Ei-l b'neigh!
B'neigh veit'kha b'karov."

A catchy tune with Hebrew lyrics, usually sung at a Passover Seder. It was about God's wonders and the hope that He would rebuild the Temple. Soon the four of us were singing along, more or less on key. Our heads were nodding along with Mr. Deutsch. We were enjoying ourselves. Tova began barking. It wasn't clear whether he was joining in or asking us to stop singing.

I drove Lottie back to her apartment feeling relieved. We agreed that a major barrier had been crossed. "You must have cast some magic spell," I said.

"It's not the first time I had to wear my folks down," Lottie said. "A year ago when Marian moved here from Albany to take the job at Addis's, she needed a roommate. I asked my parents if I could move in with her. Even though it was a short drive from their place, their first reaction was 'no', arguing that all their friends' daughters were living at home. I kept asking, pointing out that I could easily afford the rent and would stop by often. A couple of months later, to my surprise they agreed."

"So they changed their mind. Why?" I asked.

"They had second thoughts, I guess. In our case, I persuaded my mom that your personal qualities overshadowed your religious practices. And she convinced my dad. This took some time, but it seems to have worked."

"However it happened, I'm delighted," I answered.

Back home, I picked up a mystery that I had started, but I couldn't concentrate. I was preoccupied with replaying the events of the evening. I drifted off.

Color drenches the landscape -- garish greens, bright blues, blinding yellows, riotous reds. Unnatural hues. Too pristine to be real and begging to be noticed. Four of us are moving along a marked path at a fast clip, hurrying to get somewhere unknown to me. I am having trouble keeping up. I sense an animal by my feet, panting. I look down. A small dog is struggling to keep pace with his human companions. The woman in front of me is wearing a peculiar outfit, one made for a little girl, a pink-and-white flower patterned blouse, matching short skirt, and silver shoes. She turns her head, looking to the left. I know that profile, it's Lottie. She is flanked by two men. One is wearing a coat made from straw. It is shedding. Pieces are falling onto the trail like Hansel and Gretel's gumdrops. The other has on an even stranger outfit, constructed from yellow fur with a mane around his neck. They start talking. I am too far behind to make out their words, but the voices sound familiar. The one in the straw suit has a Chinese accent. Mr. Chen. The one all in yellow has a melodious, calm voice. It's Charley. Why am I falling behind them? Suddenly I realize that my clothes are heavy, making it an effort to move. I look at my arms and legs, fat, grey and with visible hinges. I hear squeaking sounds and realize it's the hinges. My vision is obstructed. I seem to be peering through a mask. I worry that I will be left behind, lumbering along, squeaking, and with just this clueless dog for company.

I call out. "Where are we going?"

"New York City."

Chapter 8: The King of Jazz

"Charley, this man you'll be meeting later sounds interesting."

I read aloud Nevin Busch's New Yorker profile of Paul Whiteman. "At 300 pounds he has a presence. A man flabby, virile, quick, coarse, untidy and sleek."

Charley half-listened as he rummaged through his tie drawer. He'd snagged an audition with the band leader and was hoping for support from his big brother.

Charley looked in the mirror as he began tying his selection, a red and navy stripe. "Well, Whiteman started as a string man. At least we have that in common."

"And Grofe recommended you. That'll help."

I was back in New York at Charley's request. He was nervous. And for good reason. Paul Whiteman was not just another Manhattan band leader, but a legend. The 'King of Jazz'. A title jazz purists rejected since improvisation, a key part of jazz performance, was nowhere in his scripted and carefully rehearsed performances. Charley loved improvising, but not for fully orchestrated pieces like Whiteman's. Every note was right there, on paper, for the performer to follow. In place of spontaneity, there were original harmonies and alternating tempos and key changes.

Improvisation, Charley thought, and I agreed, only worked for small bands. Players could look at each other and take turns exploring the music. Like friends having a conversation around a table. Such conversations would be drowned in the big bands that Whiteman directed. Charley had long admired Whiteman's skill at making music that was polished, precise and symphonic, but sounded like jazz. He relished the opportunity to audition for the King.

"Morey," he said later, "it was something out of a Hollywood movie. I was nervous as hell with Whiteman listening. I played a few bars of Whispering. He listened with no reaction. Then he stood up and signaled for me to stop. I froze." 'Do you know Fascinatin' Rhythm?' "I said I did and played some. Again he asked me to stop and began peppering me with questions about who I'd studied with, who I'd been playing with in New York, and how I knew Grofe."

'Ferde was right. You've got talent, young man. I want you to be the banjo player for my Romance in Rhythm group. You'll be at the Submarine Grill at the Traymore in Atlantic City.'

"He called in his assistant Eddie, and they signed me up. I start in three weeks."

*****

The next day we were at the Hotel Astor on Broadway well before any of the other band members. Charley was working with Carl Fenton, who like Whiteman was a top notch band leader. He went onto the stage, took out his banjo, tuned it up, and started to practice.

This scene was vintage Charley. While I might have practiced some of the numbers in my room that afternoon and showed up just before the job, Charley made sure that he was at the venue early, giving him enough time to practice for an hour or more.

"I want to get the lay of the land," he'd say, "and hear how my playing sounds in the room. It calms me down, and I think I play better."

An hour later clusters of well-heeled Manhattanites began arriving, along with their chatter and laughter. Fenton's orchestras could be counted on to draw a crowd. The noise subsided as Fenton stepped onto the bandstand and the melodic strains of Whispering filled the room. Perfection. Some in the audience smiled and began swaying along. This orchestra was a smooth music making unit. Now I could see why Charley had moved to the City: to play with the best.

On the second number, Oh, Lady Be Good, Charley started in on his solo. I was transfixed. His fingers flew over the strings, attacking the number with passion. Not just his hands, but his whole body, shoulders, head, legs and feet were making music. He even did a bit of improvising, weaving in lines from other numbers -- like Gershwin's Fascinatin' Rhythm -- that might have been showy in the hands of a less able performer. I looked around and noticed nods of approval and overheard someone ask, "What's his name?"

Benny Kruger, a friend of Charley's who had come by to hear him play, leaned toward me and whispered, "Morey, Charley's got it." He paused. Then continued,

"I've heard that other banjo players in the City would come to hear him and wonder where he got his technique. Some have even asked him what strings and picks he uses, as if that might make them play better."

By the end of the night Charley was drained, drenched in sweat, his hair matted. He knew he had performed well, and I had never seen him happier.

I stayed in the city for a couple more days, hoping it would give me a chance to watch Charley write. He had been working on a song he called No One Else Will Do, Dear. He had found a sheet of manuscript paper someone had left on the bandstand at the Biltmore with some notes written on it. He studied it, played a few bars, liked how they sounded, and from that fragment developed an idea for a song. On the spot he wrote out the entire chorus. Returning to his room, he developed it further, composing a verse and lyrics.

He told me that not a day went by that songs were not flowing into his head. He spoke of "snatching them from the air." Some flowed right out, not holding his interest. Others stayed. He would then hear variations of them, sometimes slower, sometimes faster, and in different rhythms or in other keys. His lack of formal training in composition didn't seem to matter. He knew almost instinctively how to go from a single line of melody to a nearly complete orchestration. He was savvy (and ambitious) enough, however, to know that he needed a professional arranger. That would come later.

I sat across from him in the front room and watched him compose. He would begin by striking a chord on the banjo, humming a melody, stopping and jotting down the notes on manuscript paper. He continued this way until the chorus was finished. His middle strains, from the 16th to the 24th measure, reminded me of Gershwin, unconventional and original. Later, he would return to the melody and rework it, making it sound familiar but somehow different. When he was finished with the initial draft of a number he would play it through. I could tell, just by his facial expressions what parts he liked and which ones he didn't. He would then work on the parts he wasn't happy with, trying a few variations to find one he liked. He had developed a kind of code -- pluses, minuses, checks and circles -- which he entered on the side of the sheet, indicating which sections were o.k. and which he needed to work on later.

We ran through that newborn No One Else Will Do, Dear, Charley on the banjo and me on the violin. It was the first of many duets we would play. He cautioned me never to perform any of his tunes except when we were playing them together because he worried that other musicians would try to take credit for his work. He would copyright any tune that he thought had possibilities. It was around this time that I took on the role of advisor. He trusted me. Old concerns of being treated like an outsider that had surfaced during my first visit dissipated. Charley became the creative force, I the cheerleader, and together we made music.

Chapter 9: Hot Strings

Since arriving in the City, Charley had been playing on an Iucci -- a decent enough banjo -- reliable, but unremarkable. A study in brown. The base and the neck were plain, almost drab. It was a serviceable instrument that had seen a lot of wear. In Charley's hands it made good music, but he was ready for something better.

He was performing at the Biltmore with another banjo player who had just bought a Paramount Leader Special for $350. He'd played a couple of jobs with it but didn't like its sound. "Too tinny," he'd said. Charley picked it up, played a few chords and offered to take it in return for his Iucci and $100. To his surprise the musician agreed, and Charley had as new banjo. The Paramount was a beauty.

When I first saw it, I thought it must have come from a museum. Gold plating surrounded the drum, and there was mother of pearl inlaid work along the neck. On the back the dark wood shone, as if demanding to be noticed. It was set off by two thin bands of lighter wood that ran around the drum and up the neck. A single line of the lighter wood bisected the drum, a dramatic touch. It was a heavy instrument with a big sound, crafted for a professional musician. Charley would play on it for the rest of his career.

A steady job with a name orchestra and now a new high-end instrument to call his own. That would be enough for most musicians, but Charley had bigger ambitions. He wanted to have his music published so that it could be heard by a wider audience.

*****

April found me back in New York plotting with Charley on how to find a publisher. He had already written and scored a tune called Hot Strings, but wanted something else to bring along. I had heard him play a catchy tune on the piano at the Club Colle that reminded me of a song we'd sung in school, Reuben, Reuben. It gave me an idea:

"Why not write a hot violin solo in hick style? As if a farmer suddenly discovered how to play hot double stops. And then carry that hick strain throughout the piece."

"Not a bad idea," Charley said. "Let me try it out on the piano."

Soon he had finished the solo for a number he called Hickville Hot. He had asked a pianist friend, Irv Rosenbloom, who played with George Hall's orchestra, to write the piano accompaniment. Now the piece was ready to peddle. George Engel, manager of Irving Berlin's Music Company, agreed to listen to the solos. Charley, Irv and I were ushered downstairs into a large studio where several men, including Mr. Engel, were gathered. We played the pieces for the group. When we finished Engel said, "We could use a lot of the stuff you have in your solos, but I think you need to build them up more."

"What is there to build up?" Charley asked. "They are complete already."

One of the other men who had heard the pieces approached Charley and confided, "Those numbers are very good, but you should take them to a house that goes in for more novelty tunes."

Novelty tunes. Visibly disappointed Charley replied, "Maybe I'll break up the pieces and use the strains for other songs."

"Listen," I said. "Before you turn them into spare parts, let's go down the street to Triangle Publishing with these to see if they're interested."

"Alright, but no more 'tryouts'."

By the time we arrived at the Roseland Building, Charley was his old self, a crack salesman prepared to sell his wares. He asked to see the manager. Alone. A half hour later he came out of the building wearing a smile and without the sheet music.

"They are as good as sold," he reported.

The Triangle manager had sent him downstairs to meet Alfred Hasse, head of Alfred and Company. Hasse looked at the solos, sat down at his piano and played a few bars. Swiveling around to Charley he'd said, "We have been looking for this kind of music, I'd like to publish as many of these as you can write."

Fortuitously, Henri Klickmann, who arranged all of Alfred's work, was down the hall from Hasse. Hasse called Klickmann in and asked him to look them over.

The arranger also liked what he saw, describing them as "wonderful" and began working on them that day.

Arriving back in the apartment Charley phoned Frances. Hearing his end of the conversation, I guessed that Shirley, my six-year old niece, had answered the phone.

"Yes, I'm calling from New York and Uncle Morey is with me," Charley explained. "And I'm sorry that Mimi has been whining all afternoon. We have some news to share with your mom. Is she home?"

Grinning, he started talking with Frances. "I sold two songs today, Sis. It's with Alfred and Company. One of the best." After a few minutes Charley handed me the phone. "Hi, Sis. Yes, it's great news. Not bad for a boy from Syracuse," I said.

Frances began peppering me with questions that she hadn't asked Charley. "How much will they pay him? Will he get money upfront and will there be royalties? He sold two, but how many more do you think they'll buy? Oh, and what kind of operation is Alfred and Company? Who else has published with them? Are they well known?"

As soon as I answered one question, she fired another. My sister was the practical one, Charley and I were the dreamers. Yet we were all elated with Charley's success. Frances, Charley and me: the Three Musketeers.

Our next stop was Mr. Chen's. Father and son were in, preparing for the midweek dinner crowd. William was setting out plates and glasses while Mr. Chen was helping his wife in the kitchen. "I'm now a published songwriter," Charley announced, almost shouting, as he walked in. Stopping, he put his hands on his hips, cocked his head and said, "What do you think of that?"

William stopped working, Mr. Chen put down his cleaver, and Mrs. Chen wiped her hands on her apron. All three rushed up to Charley, their questions running together like songs in different tempos playing simultaneously. It was Frances in triplicate. "Slow down, guys," Charley said, "and I'll fill you in on the details."

Of course we stayed for dinner, and Charley agreed to teach William Hot Strings the next day.

Chapter 10: Frances Weighs In

A ringing phone greeted me. Dropping my luggage and fumbling with my keys, I managed to answer on the fifth ring. It was Frances.

"Welcome back, Morey. Did you have a good trip?"

"Charley and I had a ball," I said.

"Great. I want to hear all about how he's doing. Come by for dinner tonight."

"Well as soon as I unpack, I'm off to the hotel for the night shift. What about tomorrow?"

"That'll work."

"See you then, Sis."

Shirley answered the door. "Hi, Uncle Morey. Mom's in the kitchen." Six years old, but I could already picture her as a future Frances. She had her mother's features and light brown wavy hair. She even had her walk, her heels never seeming to touch the ground as she moved across the living room toward the kitchen. Mimi was sitting on a chair watching her mother and Mary assemble the meal. She was big for a four year old, nearly as tall as her older sister. She had her father's coloring and some of his features on her mother's heart shaped face. There was a pot of soup simmering on the stove, and I could smell a roast in the oven.

An aproned Frances emerged from the kitchen. "Back from the big city he comes. Joe will be home from work any minute."

Soon Joe arrived and the five of us sat down to a family meal. Frances was expecting her third child in a month and was looking larger than I had remembered from her other pregnancies. "My doctor thinks I may be early this time and that the baby will be bigger than the other two."

"Would you like a new brother or sister?" I asked my nieces.

"Either one, but a sister would be better," Shirley answered.

"A girl," Mimi said. "I hate boys."

Once the girls were put to bed, we moved to the living room.

Joe began, "Frances tells me that Charley is getting on well in New York. Playing with good bands and has just secured a publisher for his music."

"That's right," I answered. "Things are moving at a fast tempo for him. Just like some of those songs he writes."

"Well we knew he had a gift early on," Frances said, "and more ambition that all of us other Harrises combined."

"Don't forget *disciplined*," I added. "He works on his music all the time, practicing, performing, or composing."

"Morey," Frances asked, "should I be worried about him?"

"What do you mean?" I asked.

"Well, if he works all the time, does he get enough sleep, eat properly, and socialize outside of his musician friends?"

Joe added, "What Frances means by that is, 'Is he dating anyone?'"

"Not that I know of," I answered. "There's no girl in his life."

Frances could be on to something. Charley's single mindedness had the merits of propelling his career forward, but at what cost? Having Lottie in my life gave me some perspective; I cared about someone and someone cared about me. By not having anyone to take his mind off his work, my brother might be stumbling into an unbalanced life, missing out on the perks of being an eligible bachelor in a city teeming with beautiful young women.

"I'd feel better if he found someone. Look how much happier you are with Lottie. So tell me about that contract."

"Well, Alfred and Company is a reputable publisher," I said. "I wasn't in the room, but Charley tells me that he negotiated directly with Alfred Hasse, the owner. They bought two numbers, Hickville Hot and Hot Strings on the spot. He plans to finish a number he's calling Some Fiddlin and bring it to them next week. Henri Klickmann, a terrific arranger, works for Hasse and is already working on the two pieces."

"That sounds promising. Have you seen the contract?" Frances asked.

"No, I haven't," I said, "but Charley's learned a lot since moving away. I doubt he'll be swindled."

"Alright, Morey," she said. "But I expect you to keep me posted on how it all works out. Remember, Charley has only the three of us to look out for him."

"Maybe I can help," Joe offered. "When Charley gets the contract, I'll be happy to look it over. And maybe even show it to our firm's lawyer."

"Good idea," Frances said, beaming at Joe. And I had to agree.

*****

Four days later I had my second home cooked meal of the week. Lottie had invited me over for a roast chicken served with noodle kugel, the latter dish made from her mother's recipe. I had seconds on everything.

'You can cook for me anytime, honey," I said.

"Thanks. I think I am getting better each time I try."

I filled her in about my visit with Charley.

"It sounds as if your being there helped move him along. I wonder if he could have done it all on his own," Lottie offered.

"I hadn't thought about it. You may be right," I said. "But remember, Charley has the talent and drive. I'm more of the sounding board."

"Don't underestimate your contribution. No one else in that big city cares about him like you do."

"By the way, do you think Frances is on to something about Charley not dating?" I asked.

"Maybe," she answered. "Why not raise the question when you see him next?"

At five in the morning the phone rang. And this time Joe was on the other end.

"Morey, good news. You are an uncle for the third time. An hour ago Frances delivered a healthy girl, six pounds five ounces. We named her Barbara. Mother and daughter are doing fine."

"That's wonderful. When can I see her?"

"Come by later. Crouse Irving, Room 324."

Shirley and Mimi were there when I arrived, leaning over the basinet, trying without success to get their new sister's attention. The room was far too small to hold the six of us, but I managed to move a chair aside and peek over Shirley's shoulder.

"Isn't it perfect that she's a girl, Uncle Morey?" Shirley exclaimed.

Baby Barbara was beautifully formed, plump with medium dark skin and black hair, a Russian doll come to life.

Unlike Joe, rumpled and sleep deprived, Frances looked relaxed, as if she had just strolled in from her back porch. "They're keeping me here until Tuesday. Can you believe it?" Frances asked. "If I had my way, I'd go home tomorrow."

"Has anyone called Charley yet?" I asked.

"Joe did, and he's coming in later this week to meet the baby," Frances said.

"Wonderful! It's been ages since he's been Upstate."

"Girls," I said, "Your mother and father need some time alone, so I'm taking you to lunch."

"Whee," they said in unison. "You're the bestest uncle in the world."

Chapter 11: A Sour Note

"Train 430 arriving on Track 6," the voice on the loudspeaker announced at the Vanderbilt Square Station. Waiting on the platform I noticed that the passengers leaving the train were straight from a Manhattan street corner; they were garbed in trendy, well- tailored outfits. A striking contrast to the waiting locals. There was Charley in a dark suit, bag in one hand and banjo case in the other. A study in black. He spied me and smiled. We hugged and walked to the car.

"Why did you bring the banjo?" I asked. "Planning on giving the baby some lessons?"

He smiled. "Very funny. I thought we could find a group to play with while I'm here."

"Well," I answered, "I have a job this Sunday with the Moonlight Serenaders. I think we could use a decent banjo man."

"Just 'decent'?"

*****

Beaming, Frances and Joe carried Barbara onto the Temple Concord bimah. The baby naming began. Rabbi Friedman recited a blessing to welcome her into the community. Holding Barbara aloft, he announced her Hebrew name, "Basha bat Josef. May your life be a blessing to your family and to this congregation."

After the service, Frances reprised her working the room routine. Her brother in tow, she approached guests with: "You remember my brother Charley. In from New York." Her words echoing the way she'd introduced Lottie months earlier. Lottie had been caught off guard, but Charley wasn't. He wouldn't expect anything different from his always-in-control older sister. Charley didn't seem to mind. He enjoyed the attention, even beamed when some of the crowd recognized him. A few, who knew about his move to New York, asked how his career was going. I trailed along behind him like a background accompanist. Unlike Charley I was no novelty, more like an often-heard tune.

Back at the house, we admired the baby. Up close she was even prettier than at the hospital -- a plump creature with a full face, large eyes and dark hair. "Who does she take after?" we all wondered. Frances thought it was our father, Joe thought his mother, I thought Frances, and Charley said she just looked like any other baby.

At Joe's insistence, Charley had mailed him a copy of his Alfred and Company contract.

"Our lawyer is meeting with us tomorrow at 1:00," Joe said.

"Well, Ferde Grofe and some others already looked it over. They said it was fine." He paused then added, "But I suppose another set of eyes can't hurt."

The next day we met Lottie at Schrafft's on East Warren Street. It was her lunch hour and Addis's was nearby. She had missed the baby naming, but wanted to see Charley while he was in town. We had agreed to not bore her with talk about our music. Lottie was anxious to hear Charley's take on life as a New Yorker.

"Charley," she began, "Morey may have told you that I don't plan to stay here forever. I want to be a store manager or buyer, and New York offers better opportunities."

"I can't advise you on that score," he said, "but I will say that New York gets under your skin. The kind of place that once you're settled in, you never want to leave."

He went on about the city's merits, sprinkling in a few of its shortcomings along the way. After a bit I realized that Charley hadn't just moved downstate to pursue a career. He had crossed an ocean, akin to our grandfather's voyage from England to America. A one way trip from the Old World to the New.

Lottie listened, fully engaged. She sat forward, taking little notice of her salad, her head nodding as Charley continued with his monologue.

"I want to hear more, but my lunch hour is over. Thanks for the Manhattan tour."

I kissed Lottie and watched her leave the restaurant, her heels making a rapid click, click cadence.

Charley and I walked a few blocks to South Clinton Street. Joe's sprawling office took up most of the State Tower building's third floor. Entering Joe's office I saw that Manny Feldman, the company lawyer, was already looking over Charley's contract. Joe introduced us.

Manny began, "Charley, Joe might have mentioned that I'm a corporate not a copyright lawyer. I called a friend in New York who is and read him the agreement."

I glanced at Charley. A frown darkened his face. I wondered why.

"I thought, and my friend concurred, that you have a pretty good deal here."

"Right," Charley said.

"Yes, Alfred has a good reputation. They gave you a decent advance and you get to keep thirty percent of the profits from the sheet music sales. They're running an initial printing of a thousand copies with distribution to stores in the East Coast and Chicago. Not bad for an unknown composer. I doubt that you'll become a rich man from these sales, but I am assuming that's not what you want."

"Well for now I just want to get my name out there. Have bands play my music."

"Are there more pieces in the works?"

"I'm writing all the time. So I guess the answer is 'yes'."

Turning to Joe, Manny said: "Good for Charley. Small town boy makes it in the big city."

Joe and I thanked Manny, and then Charley and I left. Charley was silent. When we reached the street he stopped abruptly and began ranting.

"Why was that meeting necessary? Joe and Manny must think me an idiot. I'm in the music business. There're not. I don't need their two cents."

And on he went, like a frenetic jazz riff going on too long.

"Joe has a tin ear. Manny probably can't even read music. Neither one could tell Dixieland from Blues if their life depended on it."

He had started walking aimlessly, cutting a serpentine path and gesturing wildly all the while. His face flushed, and a vein I had never noticed appeared on his right temple.

I tried reasoning with him. "You realize that you just got some pricey legal advice for free. Show some appreciation."

"Baloney. That lawyer had to call New York to figure out what I already knew. Typical boonies lawyer, in way over his head. And why did Joe butt in to begin with? I knew my contract was solid."

"I'm sure Frances asked him. And he wanted to do his wife a favor."

That left him speechless. Criticizing Frances, a Madonna-like figure in our eyes, was off limits for both of us. Finally, he settled down, pouting.

In a flash my brother had gone from calm to crazy, as if a familiar mountain you thought was benign erupted, spewing lava everywhere. With little provocation, arrogance and distain replaced civility. Who is this new Charley? Was it the year in New York rubbing elbows with talented competitors on the make that had changed him? Or was this darker side already there, just waiting to surface?

Charley never sat in on the hotel gig. He took an early train back to the City.

Chapter 12: After the Storm

The next day Frances phoned. "Is Charley there? I want to wish him a safe trip."

"He decided to leave early." Trying to sound nonchalant, I added, "I think he needs to get ready for a job."

She paused, taking it in. "Oh. That's odd. Why didn't he call me then?"

"You know our brother. It's all about his career."

"At least he came in to meet his new niece."

I knew my sister well enough to know that she had figured it out. Joe had probably reported on our meeting with his lawyer, noting that Charley had left abruptly, dispensing with the usual niceties. She was waiting for me to say more, but I demurred, needing some time to figure out what Charley was up to.

I was in a funk. Maybe a drink would help. I rooted around in the back of the cupboard and found an ancient bottle of Jim Beam. Dusting it off, I poured a glass, picked up some sheet music for an upcoming job with the Moonlight Serenaders, and settled into my favorite chair.

The whiskey warmed my throat. I poured a second glass and felt my whole body relax. After a bit, I dozed off.

I'm holding my violin. Tuning it up, getting ready to practice a new piece. To lose myself in thoughts of the music I'll make. The black chin piece feels good against my face, and the bow becomes an extension of my arm, natural. I slide the bow across the first string, it's flat. A quarter turn on the screw. I try again. Good. The sweet sound of a perfect G. I move on to the other strings, adjusting each one in turn. I pause, shake out my arm and begin caressing the strings with my bow. I stop. The G string is out of tune again. I adjust it and start over. Now it's the F string. Flat. I turn the screw. Now the D string is off. My playing sounds like the screechy noises I made when I first picked up a violin decades ago. My head throbs. Another round of tuning. Nothing works.

Trial and error. Error and error. Soon my head is pounding. I start swearing. Cursing at the instrument. Then I swing the bow above my head. Wildly, like a cowboy with a lasso. I work myself into a frenzy. Sweating. I drop the bow and grab the instrument with both hands. Cursing it. I walk over to the other end of the room, stopping by the mirror. I see my reflection. I look crazed. Eyes red. Hair askew. It's me, but not me. I bang the violin against the wall. It leaves a black streak on the grey wall, but nothing happens. I try again. Bang. Bang. Crack. The back splits open. Success.

I drop the crippled instrument. Stomp on it with my bare feet. Cursing. It breaks into shards of polished wood. A splinter lodges in the arch of my right foot. Searing pain. I hobble into the bathroom, a trail of blood marking my path. Inexplicably, I am greeted by a lineup of items belonging in a hospital: alcohol, bandages, tape, cotton swabs. I sit on the toilet, remove the splinter and bandage my foot.

Back in my room, I locate a large paper bag and begin picking up the violin pieces. First the larger ones -- the neck with its splayed strings, the ones that refused to be tuned, followed by pieces of the back and sides of what was once a pristine creation that made music.

I spot the bow. I think about cracking it over my knee, but am in too much pain to bother. I stand on my good foot, lay the bow on top of the dresser, and settle back into bed, trying to ignore the pulsing pain.

Voices outside my window woke me. I was still in the chair, sheet music in my lap. I jumped up, reassured that my feet were fine. My pulse racing, I located my violin case and snapped it open. The instrument gleamed back at me, unscratched. Pristine. The bow rested comfortably beside it. I exhaled and calmed down.

I crossed the room toward the mirror, seeking reassurance that my appearance hadn't changed. I looked the same, except for a tuft of hair out of place. I picked up a brush and ran it through my hair. As I put it down I noticed something to the right of the mirror: two long black marks on the grey wall. They weren't there yesterday. They stared back at me like two silent screams.

Chapter 13: Silent Interlude

Siblings drift in and out of each other's lives. A brother might move from his hometown to take a new job or go off to war or a sister might move after marrying. These separations are commonplace, predictable, and normal. Despite them siblings usually maintain their relationship, reaffirming the importance of blood ties.

Not in our story, for the ties between Charley and me were frayed. Perhaps torn beyond repair.

When we were young our mother would play a game she called "Imagine". She would describe a room and ask us to imagine how it was furnished, asking the player to describe an object in detail, including where it was located. The next player would have to name another object that was linked with it ("brown wooden side table next to the red upholstered armchair.") A variation on the game was for us to **not** imagine something, like "Imagine there is no elephant in front of our house." This twist proved to be a far greater challenge, one we never mastered.

Some days were like Mother's variation of the game, as I tried to not think about Charley. It never worked. My stomach muscles would tighten, and I could feel my blood pressure rise.

Frances, who spoke with Charley often, would fill me in on his life in New York. When I feigned disinterest she would suggest that he was asking about me. Of course I knew he wasn't. And she knew that I knew. It was her way of trying to shrink the gulf between us. She maintained I had overreacted to the meeting with Joe and Manny, claiming that even they had excused Charley's rudeness as the behavior of a "young and temperamental artist."

Well, I was not as charitable. I believed Charley was deliberately distancing himself from his family and hometown. Like a snake shedding its skin, my brother was discarding his old self and taking on a new one. This "new" Charley slithered through a landscape of fellow musicians who, like him, were talented, ambitious, and cocky.

Not that this was a surprise. It had been foreshadowed during my July visit. Lou and Ross had known all about Charley's jobs and compositions while I was left out in the cold. Only a year earlier Charley had been sharing his work with me and seeking my advice. But he never mentioned that he knew Grofe, for example, and, even after we met him at the Gershwin performance, failed to clarify their relationship.

His blowup after our meeting with Joe and Manny and his abrupt departure for New York brought into bold relief what I had already suspected: he was moving on. He didn't need us. Me.

I worked hard on eliminating Charley from my thoughts. I dove into my weekly routine, turning down dinner invitations from Frances. I wanted to avoid the inevitable questions about when Charley and I were planning to "start acting like brothers again."

My disenchantment with Charley spilled over to his adopted city. Whatever pull Manhattan had had for me faded. I now saw my hometown through fresh eyes. Sure, opportunities for talented musicians in New York were plentiful and more lucrative, but there were jobs Upstate too. The air in Manhattan was foul and the living quarters close. Even a walk was a challenge; crowds filled the sidewalks and crossing a street meant avoiding speeding cars while stepping around horse droppings.

Syracuse, in contrast, was a comfortable place: people were friendly, majestic trees abounded, and the air was clean. The city that Charley had fled was a boom town. Syracuse made things that people actually used: telephones, engine parts, typewriters, headlights, iron and steel beams, cigars, bicycles, cabinetry, pottery, candles, and automobiles. Despite its smaller population, it produced more varied products than New York, a point that Charles Hanna, our mayor, made to anyone who would listen.

Around this time I befriended John Wilkinson. His dad, John Senior, along with Herbert Franklin had started the Franklin car company. H.H. Franklin Company was a big deal in the city. It was a major employer; the 3,500 people working there produced 15, 000 cars a year. John worked at the South Geddes Street plant, but on weekends he played piano for Jimmie Long's Orchestra and later, the Ipana Troubadours. We met on a job with Jimmie Long's group at the Hotel Onondaga and hit it off immediately.

John was a beanstalk, six foot three and bone thin. He had enormous hands and his fingers were a blur when he played, while his back and shoulders moved from side to side with the music. He was an outgoing guy who loved an audience. His girlfriend Rose was willowy, nearly as tall as John. When Lottie and I went out with them it must have looked as if they were taking their younger siblings out for the evening.

Then there were John's cars. It seemed that he had a new one every month. All Franklins. All beauties. Except for the hoods. Franklins lacked a conventional radiator, giving the front end a stubby look, like a circumcision gone awry. The passenger compartment was roomy and well crafted. When the four of us went out, John insisted on driving. A good idea since my Regal would have to struggle to accommodate the two giraffes.

Riding with John had its downside though. He was as enthusiastic about his cars as he was about making music and eager to let you know it. A ride to Green Lake would be accompanied by a sort of sales pitch:

"This model, like all our Franklins, has an air cooled, six cylinder aluminum engine. My dad's design. The automatic spark plugs are new this year. Ford has yet to figure out how to make them." He would depress the gas pedal. "Feel how smoothly she accelerates."

And, as the car burst forward pushing us back against our seats, Rose turned to Lottie and rolled her eyes, as if to say, "Here we go again."

Lottie was busy admiring the workmanship on the leather seats, running her right hand lightly over the detailed tufting. "I don't mean to be nosey, John, but if I wanted to buy this car, what would it cost?"

"Well, it lists for $3,300. But I could work out a deal for you with one of our dealers; that would bring it down to $2,900."

"Is that all? I had no idea. I'd only have to sell three hundred dresses to buy it," she laughed.

Nearly three grand, I thought. That would get me five new Buicks. Who buys these things?

I wondered how Charley might react to John and his Franklin. Unimpressed and happy that he didn't have to bother with a car in Manhattan.

But there was more to John than a love of cars. He was a talented musician and could have made music his career, but his passion was engineering. He worked only a twenty-hour week at the Franklin plant, leaving time for his classes at the university. He took his studies seriously and often brought one of his textbooks to a gig, reading and taking notes during breaks.

"John, it's the weekend. Time for relaxing and making music."

"Not every weekend, Morey."

"Do you have to drag those books around?"

"I have a quiz Monday and I want to do well on it."

"What are those classes like? Lots of incomprehensible formulas on the blackboard, I'd guess."

"There's some of that. Except that they do make sense."

I was intrigued and tried to imagine what went on in a college-level class. "Is it as hard as translating Greek?"

"Why not come to one of my classes and find out for yourself, wise guy?"

Ten days later I was in Syracuse University's Steele Hall, Room 202, listening to Professor Simpkins comparing the tensile strength of steel and aluminum. I was a decade older than most of the students and not much younger than the professor. Simpkins was a husky man wearing an ill- fitting black suit that strained from his large shoulders and arms. He had been a competitive boxer, John had said. I could see that and would not want to face him in the ring.

As I had joked, dozens of incomprehensible formulas covered the two massive blackboards in the front of the room. Professor Simpkins added even more, pressing hard on the chalk as he moved it along, leaving little clouds of chalk dust in its wake.

This was all new to me. No one in my family, except for Joe (and that was by marriage) had attended college. I had a superficial knowledge of the campus. Frances and Joe's house bordered its east side, and Lottie and I had often taken late night walks along the quad, admiring how the buildings' facades shown in the moonlight. Although I had attended a couple of organ concerts at Hendricks Chapel and cheered the Orangemen at Archibald Stadium, I had never stepped inside a classroom.

I had done well in my science and math classes at Central High, but here I had expected to be lost at sea, to not comprehend a college-level engineering lecture. To my surprise, after listening awhile I began to follow it, even finding it engaging. I borrowed some paper from John, retrieved a pen from a pocket, and began to take notes. John looked over and smiled.

College might not be such a stretch for me, I thought.

Three weeks later, my phone rang. I was just getting out of the shower. Hurrying to answer, I left a trail of wet footprints on the dark wood floor.

Chapter 14: Rhapsodona

"Morey?" An unfamiliar voice asked. "William here. William Chen. You and Charley ate in my dad's restaurant awhile back."

"Oh yes. I remember," I said as a puddle formed on the floor. "You're calling from New York?"

"That's right."

"So, William. Is everything o.k. there?" I asked, one-handedly drying water off my chest and legs.

"Yes and no." He paused. "Well, you know I see Charley every Tuesday for lessons."

"Uh huh," wondering where this was going.

"He tells me that the two of you don't talk very much."

"You could say that. But it's more like -- never. We stopped talking a long time ago." Now I was on one knee, mopping up water with the towel.

"I think Charley misses you."

"Oh, I doubt that. Would you mind if I put the phone down for a second?"

"Is this a bad time?"

"No, I just need to get something." For some reason I didn't want to continue this conversation while naked.

I went over to the bed, picked up the underwear I had laid out, put it on, and walked back to the phone.

"Still there, William? What can I do for you?"

"Actually, it's for Charley. Maybe even for you, too."

William went on for some time. He began by describing Charley as "very upset" that he and I weren't speaking. At first, Charley had felt that our mutual silence was my fault, since I had failed to see how condescending to the Syracuse crowd could help his career. Later he'd had a change of heart, admitting that he might have had something to do with the situation, yet uncertain what to do about it.

Mr. Chen told William that Charley had even sought his advice, seeing him as a neutral party and surrogate parent.

"Be the bigger man," he had told Charley. "Call Morey and apologize."

Charley hadn't been happy with that advice and wasn't ready to act on it.

When William later saw how Charley was torn, he had decided to take charge.

"So, Morey, Dad and I are inviting you to come down here. Rudy Vallee is going to premier a number that Charley wrote."

"Uh huh."

"It'll be at the Warwick on the 15th. I think Charley would like you to hear it. You can stay with us. What do you say?"

"I don't know."

"If you want, I can run interference."

I smiled at that.

Ten days later I stepped again into Grand Central's cavernous hall. William was there, gazing at the ceiling, just as I had done months earlier.

"Amazing! Such a clever way to decorate a ceiling. Maybe we can copy it for the restaurant."

"I doubt it would work," I said curtly, in no mood for ceiling discussion.

As we walked through Mr. Chen's front door, familiar aromas greeted me, whetting my appetite. It was midafternoon, and I realized I had had nothing to eat since breakfast. Lunch service was over, and the waiters were polishing glasses and changing the linens. Mrs. Chen turned off her vacuum cleaner and greeted me warmly.

"Mowree. Good to see you. You stay with us. Right?"

"Looking forward to it."

"I make you some lunch. William will bring it up."

William led me to the back of the room, snaking through clusters of tables that had been moved to accommodate the vacuuming. Holding my bag in front of me, I threaded up the narrow stairway to the second floor. Once in the apartment, I noticed that the layout there mirrored the restaurant's narrow footprint, with rooms laid out end-to-end like cars on a railroad train. The living room led to the dining room, with an apartment sized kitchen to one side. The bedrooms were arranged in a row behind that with the guest room in the caboose position. I put my bag on the bed.

A few minutes later I settled into my seat at the round wooden dining table. Mrs. Chen had prepared egg drop soup and its aroma filled my nostrils. William had already started on his bowl.

"I'm learning a lot from Charley," he offered between slurps.

"That's nice," I said flatly.

"At first Dad was against the idea. 'None of that colored music in our house' he would say. He wanted me to follow my sister and study the old masters. Play Bach and Mozart."

"What changed his mind?" This was starting to get interesting.

"Charley. It was the way he talked to Dad about jazz, explaining that it was not just loud noise, but music. 'Sure, Mozart is timeless, but Gershwin is timely' he would say. He even played a few bars, comparing them."

"And it worked?"

"Yup. Although I think it was because Charley charmed Dad rather than the music converting him."

"What about you?" I asked, reaching for an egg roll. "Why the banjo?"

"Oh. I always liked Duke Ellington. I have a bunch of his records, and when I heard Fred Guy's banjo solo on Immigration Blues, I was hooked. What a sound!"

"So you started looking for a teacher?"

"Not really. A while back I waited on Charley and his buddies and noticed his banjo case. We started talking, and he offered to give me lessons."

"And the rest is history," I chuckled.

"Kind of. Lessons in trade for meals. I have the better end of the deal, but don't tell Charley," he said, grinning.

"Not a chance, since we're not speaking."

*****

The Warwick hostess showed William and me to a table near the back of the room. Charley's roommate Ross was already there. He greeted us and handed me a program. The orchestra would be playing familiar tunes: Did You Ever See a Dream Walking, All Aboard for Heaven, and Moonlight Madness. But in the middle of the playlist was a new tune:

Rhapsodona, composed by C. Harris

My eyes widened. I remembered a conversation Charley and I had had before our break. He was enamored with Gershwin's Rhapsody in Blue, calling it a 'brilliant piece with a perfect title'. I agreed. To a musician 'rhapsody' means a free form, or a composition that breaks from a conventional structure. "One day," he had said, "I would like to write my own rhapsody."

And now he had done it. The title had a special meaning, based on a story I had suggested: A Spanish noblewoman embarks on an affair with a commoner. At first it's all about passion, but when the affair is revealed, she is rejected by her family and peers. Charley added 'dona', the Spanish world for noblewoman, to the end of 'rhapsody'. Rhapsodona. The perfect title.

As the final strains of All Aboard for Heaven played, Rudy Vallee turned to the audience:

"We have a special treat. A promising young musician, Charley Harris, is sitting in with us this evening."

Vallee pointed to Charley, gesturing for him to stand. Charley set his banjo aside, stood, and bowed his head to light applause.

"Charley has just published a song titled Rhapsodona. We will perform it for the first time, here on our stage. I hope you enjoy it."

Lou Raderman, Vallee's first violinist, stood and walked center stage while Frank Longo sat down at the keyboard. The duet began and the sound of romance filled the room. The piece was nothing like Charley's "hot jazz" numbers. This one was written in a fox trot tempo, lyrical and romantic. It was an original, yet here and there I heard echoes of Gershwin. A charming piece, well performed by Raderman and Longo.

I glanced over at Ross, then at William. Both were swaying in time to the beat, clearly enjoying themselves. The piece ended followed by warm applause. I had a mixed reaction. While the melody, arrangement, and performance were arresting, the piece seemed incomplete. The three part story Charley and I had talked about was nowhere to be heard. The piece conveyed romance, even passion, but not its consequences. It was truncated, like a one act play. I wondered why Charley had dropped the original plan. But then again Rudy Vallee thought enough of the number to showcase it here.

Intermission. I watched Charley as he stood and walked down from the stage toward our table looking for Ross and William. As soon as he saw me he stopped, turned around, and stalked back toward the stage. How petty, I thought. Too proud to even greet me. He crossed the now empty stage to the piano, sat down, picked up some sheet music and began writing.

A few moments later he appeared at our table. "Morey, what a surprise. How did you know about this?"

"I invited him," William interjected.

I fixed my eyes on Charley. My expression cold. "I wasn't sure I'd come, but he was very persuasive."

Ignoring my tone, Charley replied, "Well...Thanks for coming. Here. I have something for you..."

It was the sheet music for Rhapsodona, the cover printed in red, blue and black with Charley's picture below the title. The Devil danced across a violin in the center of the page, and in the upper right hand corner Charley had written:

To Maurice Vann,
My Best Pal and Brother
Chas Saul Harris

Chapter 15: Chinatown, My Chinatown

William woke me early the next morning, a Sunday, the one day I usually sleep in.

"Rise and shine, Morey. Time to get moving."

"Moving?" I growled, "What do you have in mind?"

"A trip downtown. To meet the family."

"The family?"

"Yup. The Chinatown branch."

Chinatown? Never thought I would visit the place. I dressed, recalling a familiar song:

Chinatown, my Chinatown,
Where the lights are low,
Hearts that know no other land,
Drifting to and fro.
Dreamy, dreamy Chinatown,
Almond eyes of brown,
Hearts seem light and
Life seems bright
In dreamy Chinatown.

Corny lyrics grafted onto a catchy tune. I'd played it dozens of times, fox trot tempo, while watching couples mouth the words as they glided across the dance floor. Now I would be off to the real place, not the one from Jerome and Schwartz's imagination.

It's bound to be bigger than the two-block one in Syracuse, I thought. Beyond that I had no idea what to expect.

The Chens and daughter Susan sat near the front, while William and I stood in the middle of the subway car. Hands on straps, we swayed from side-to-side, in synch with the rhythm of the train. William, straining to be heard over the din of the train's rumble, began filling me in on the story of the "Chen Clan."

"My granddad came over in 1860, just before they closed the door on immigrants. He had studied at Peking University, but knew he would never find work in China and hoped that he had a better chance here. His older brother, who was already in New York, sponsored him, even found him a job."

"Doing what?"

"Menial labor. But Granddad had a plan."

"A restaurant?"

"Yup. And a few years later, with help from his family he had cobbled together enough funds to build it. The original Mr. Chen's was a couple of blocks from here. And it did pretty well."

"When did it move?"

"Oh. That was Dad's doing. He wanted his new place to be uptown, not down here. Thought he would have less competition in a neighborhood where not every business had dead ducks hanging in the front window," he added with a smile.

"And your mom, when did he meet her?"

"They grew up together. Here in Chinatown. Their families lived a block apart. They opened the business together, back in '14. She cooked, he was the businessman."

I was about to ask about Mr. Chen's uncle when William said:

"Here's our stop."

We climbed the Mott Street station stairs and stepped into another world: noisy, colorful, and teeming with life. A dense crowd carried us along as I struggled to stay on the narrow sidewalk, trying to avoid the street thick with cars, horses and pushcarts. William led the way, his long legs and spare frame moving him nimbly through the crowded landscape. Undeterred, as if he were strolling through an open field. Susan stayed by my side, guiding me along, while the elder Chens lagged behind.

I looked over my shoulder, searching for them. There they were, standing outside a dry goods shop chatting with another couple. Animated and smiling, they appeared to be in no hurry to reach our destination. This world, so alien to me, was their home. I wondered if they felt like outsiders in their uptown restaurant surrounded by Caucasians.

A few blocks later the crowd thinned a bit. William crossed a narrow street and knocked on a colorfully painted door. Susan and I followed, arriving just as an older man, who bore a striking resemblance to Mr. Chen, opened the apartment door and greeted William.

Susan led me up the stairs to a large apartment. She went ahead, leaving me in the hallway. I could hear voices in a nearby room, people talking over one another. A young girl, not more than four or five, stared in my direction. A stylishly dressed young woman, who I assumed was her mother, took her hand. They walked toward me.

"You must be Morey. William said you might be joining us. I am Christine, William's cousin." The child tugged on her mother's skirt. "And this is my daughter, Lottie."

"Nice to meet you both," I smiled at the coincidence that a youngster in Chinatown would share a name with my girlfriend. Small world indeed.

"Lottie. Is that short for something?"

"No. Just 'Lottie'. When her father saw her for the first time he said that she was 'as beautiful as a Lotus blossom'."

Christine looked down at her daughter and winked. "We couldn't call you 'Lotus', could we? But 'Lottie' made sense."

"I like my name a whole lot. This much." Lottie said, spreading her arms wide.

"Me too," I said. "And guess what?"

"What?"

"You and my girlfriend have the exact same name."

"Oh!" Lottie said as she scampered away.

Abandoning the hallway, I stepped into the living room. It was an all-male domain. The men were huddled in groups of three or four, talking rapidly and gesturing. Not understanding anything, I focused on the sounds. The words were in a minor key and spoken in rat-tat-tat fashion. The energy in the room was palpable, suggesting that important topics were being covered. If only I knew what they were saying.

Aromas from an adjoining kitchen drew me. I walked to the doorway and peeked in. Nearly a dozen women filled the modest-sized room. They were busy preparing lunch while carrying on animated conversations that rivaled those in the neighboring room, but an octave higher. Though standing shoulder-to-shoulder, each woman attended to her task -- chopping, cooking, or assembling dishes -- without bumping into a neighbor. Every so often they rotated, in unison, counterclockwise, when one of the crew needed to change stations, to add something to a wok or to plate a dish. Steam from the stove bathed the cooks. The effect was ethereal, a scene from a ballet when the troupe dances in a circle. I almost expected to hear Tchaikovsky in the background.

A hand on my elbow led me back to the living room. It was William.

"Morey, lunch isn't ready yet. Come meet more of the family."

By the end of the day I had met nearly two dozen friends and members of the Chen family. Many spoke English and William translated for the ones who didn't. While most lived in Chinatown several of the younger ones were leaving, moving uptown. A few knew Charley, liked him, and seemed disappointed that he hadn't joined me. I didn't bother to mention that if he had, I wouldn't have come.

Chapter 16: Dreamy Chinatown

I was back in Syracuse and overbooked. Again. Scheduled to work the hotel's front desk, I'd also agreed to play one gig with the Troubadours on Saturday and another with the Hottentots on Sunday. And Mimi, Frances and Joe's oldest, had a fifth birthday party on Sunday that "Uncle Morey (and Aunt Lottie) just had to attend."

Busy as I was, my thoughts kept returning to New York to the Chen's hospitality and to hearing Charley's Rhapsodona. Two surprises in two days. Charley's piece turned out to be engaging, but incomplete. And then there was his note on the score. Did my brother really think that a single gesture, a few strokes of the pen, would erase the past? Or was he just taking a first step, like a toddler starting to walk, tentative, awkward, and hoping not to fall?

But thoughts of the Chens edged out those of Charley. Before that weekend I had expected a bed for a night and, perhaps, a good meal or two. I got much more.

William had introduced me to another world, one that bore little resemblance to the Chinatown of song. Far from a dreamland, it was a crowded, colorful, and bustling island within a city that was itself an island. A place where people looked different, spoke in an unfamiliar tongue, yet to whom I felt a kinship.

The Chinatowners had a lot in common with my family. Both came as immigrants who were unfamiliar with American customs. Even after Congress barred them from entering our shores, they survived. Some, like the Chens, took further risks, moving to a neighborhood that might not want them. Could they be the community's future, straddling two worlds, the "new country" uptown and the "old country" downtown?

These outsiders welcomed me, a stranger, to an intimate gathering that mirrored the ordinary ones my family held. Just as Frank Baum's Dorothy peeked behind the curtain and saw that the powerful wizard was an ordinary man, I saw that beneath its surface Chinatown was anything but "dreamy."

*****

I picked up Lottie and we went on to Mimi's party. My niece was only five and already showing signs of her mother's bossiness. She was the middle child, but seemed to run the lives of both her older and younger siblings.

My sister's living room was awash in crepe paper. A pink and green jungle. A dozen giggling five-year-olds watched as Mimi, blindfolded, was spun around three times. With a paper tail attached to a pin in her right hand she walked toward the wrong wall, one without an image of a donkey taped to it. "Go left," a blonde haired girl shouted. Mimi did, then stumbled into a floor lamp. The giggling grew louder. Mimi, now familiar with the landscape, regained her balance and headed straight for the donkey and pushed in the pin with its attached tail, right on target. Her face lit up as she pulled off the blindfold and inspected her work.

"See what I did, Aunt Lottie, Uncle Morey. Just for you!"

"Terrific. Well done," we said in unison.

Not missing a beat, Mimi introduced us to her friends in one long breath.

"This is my best friend Ellen. She lives down the street. And this is my best friend Gertie; we play dress-up together. This is my other best friend Florence. We walk to school together."

We nodded, acknowledging each introduction. By the fifth "best friend", I began planning an escape from Mimi's monologue.

"Lottie, Morey. Come into the kitchen." Frances to the rescue.

"Was my 'shy' daughter entertaining you?" Frances asked. Mary, who was finishing up decorating the birthday cake, reacted with a soprano's laugh.

"Well, she comes by her 'take charge' attitude honestly," I answered.

Frances shrugged.

Lottie offered to help set up the dining room, and I handed Mimi's gift, a set of dollhouse furniture, to Frances.

"Perfect choice, Morey, Lottie. Mimi spends hours playing house."

"I was hoping she'd like it. Is Joe around?"

"No. He's at Fred Ackerman's. Playing poker."

"Oh. I was looking forward to seeing him."

103

"Next time. Fortunately for you, I'm too busy to pester you about your trip."

"Very wise."

"But you did see Charley?"

"Yes. But I went to hear his new piece, not to stage a brothers' reunion."

After Mimi had unwrapped her presents, everyone had devoured the cake, and the last guest had left, Lottie and I sat on the back porch, sipping lemonade and enjoying the quiet. The massive elms that ringed Frances and Joe's yard lent a bit of grandeur to the scene, as if to suggest that only important things should be discussed here.

"Morey, it's been nearly a week, and you have not mentioned a thing about your trip to the City. How did it go?"

"Well, interesting, but not what I expected."

I filled her in on the highlights: the Chen's hospitality, hearing Rhapsodona, and my Chinatown excursion. She listened silently. When I finished, she gazed across the yard, appearing to fixate on a black squirrel sitting motionless on the branch of a neighboring tree. Then, when it saw something and darted off, Lottie turned to me.

"Morey, I sense that something's changed."

"How so?"

"That was not an ordinary visit."

"Go on."

"Others were about seeing Charley. This one might have started out that way, but ended up differently."

"Honey, you're right. I learned something new about the City."

"Speaking of 'something new', I have news."

"I'm all ears."

'Remember back when you and Charley were speaking and we took that trip to New York?"

"Sure do."

"I was at one of the plants on 36th Street. Helen, our buyer, and I were picking out dresses for the spring line. Well, she introduced me to Don Rubenstein, the head buyer for Bergdorf Goodman."

"Bergdorf Goodman?"

"It's a major New York retailer. Very upscale. Anyway, their business is growing and they plan to open a new store on Fifth Avenue next year. They'll need people."

"And?"

"Well, Mr. Rubenstein called me yesterday and asked me to come down for an interview on the 15th."

A moment of panic. Lottie moving two hundred miles away. Could we handle it? Regaining my composure, I congratulated her.

"Sounds promising. What's the position?"

"Assistant buyer."

"Isn't that what you are now?"

"True. But Addis's is a small retailer, Bergdorf's is moving into the big leagues. But nothing is solid," she allowed. "I am sure he's interviewing other people."

"He'd be nuts not to pick you." I said a silent prayer hoping that he wouldn't. "What do your folks say?"

"Not overjoyed. Especially Dad."
"I would expect that. I'll drive you to the station."

Chapter 17: There'll be Some Changes Made

<u>November 16th, Knickerbocker Square Station</u>

Right away I could see that Lottie was struggling to suppress a smile as she stepped off the afternoon train from Manhattan.

"Thanks for meeting me, Morey. It was hectic. I didn't have a minute to catch my breath. And I'm pooped."

"So, it went well?" I asked as I took her bags.

"Yes, it did. They really grilled me."

"Did they give you a decision?"

"Well, you're looking a Bergdorf's newest Assistant Buyer, Women's Better Dresses!"

"Congratulations, honey," I remarked, kissing her warmly.

"Thanks."

I took her bag as we left the station and walked to my car.

"When do you start?"

"After the New Year. We will be working on getting the new store up and running."

Lottie settled into the front seat next to me and began ticking off tasks, uncurling a finger with each one.

"I need to give notice at work. Get out of my lease. Find a place in Manhattan. Find a roommate or two to share the rent. Start packing."

She stopped her finger counting, looked ahead at the road and said, "But first I need to break the news to my folks that I'm moving to New York. That's the tough one."

"So, any reservations?" I said, hoping she had some.

"Not really. But it'll be a test for you and me."

I was relieved to be entered on the long list of things to worry about.

"I guess I'll be wearing down the road between here and New York come January."

December 16th, West 51st Street

John Wilkinson parked his Franklin du jour (a 1927 touring model, teal blue, black interior) behind me outside Lottie's Manhattan apartment. The three of us, Lottie and I in my Regal, and John in his Franklin, had departed Syracuse early that morning, both cars crammed with Lottie's stuff, leaving barely enough room to see out the rear windows. We had formed a little caravan; I was in front and John followed. While my Regal groaned from time-to-time as it struggled up the mountain passes, John's car, with its muscular engine, did not. It strode the hills effortlessly, like a competitive athlete. We had stopped a couple times to refuel, both the cars and us.

Lottie's apartment was on the third floor of an attractive prewar brownstone. Her new roommates, Yetta Dana and Marie Bradford, were also in the fashion business. Yetta was a floor manager at Bergdorf's, Marie a model for several stores, including Bergdorf's. I wondered how the three clothes-horses would find closet space for their extensive wardrobes.

Lottie's room was just off the front room and had two windows overlooking the street, inviting the afternoon sun to stream in. "Very charming," John said as he and I placed the last of Lottie's boxes in the room's far corner.

"Morey, why don't you and John grab a snack while I start unpacking. There's a coffee shop around the corner."

An unfamiliar voice greeted us when we returned to the apartment. A willowy blonde with a no nonsense attitude was standing over Lottie, hands on hips, helping her arrange a dresser.

Lottie introduced us. "Yetta, this is Morey, my boyfriend, and John, a friend and unpaid mover."

"Hi, fellows. Nice to meet you," Yetta said. Turning on a pivot, she went back to her task.

"I think we should put your scarves and gloves in the top drawer, like this," she announced, stepping in front of Lottie and quickly arranging her items. "And your undergarments -- they're lovely, by the way-- right here, in the next drawer."

"If you insist," Lottie said, her tone measured as she tried to hide her annoyance. Apparently the 'Yetta Takes Charge' play had been going on for a while.

Lottie turned to me, her back to Yetta and plaintively mouthed, "Save me, Morey."

"Um, Lottie, can't this wait until later? We should get over to the Chens. They're expecting us."

"You don't mind, Yetta? We can finish up after dinner."

Startled, Yetta answered: "Sure. Go ahead, kids. Have fun."

In a blur Lottie had donned her coat and was out the door. John and I followed and we piled into the Franklin.

"Thanks for saving me from Yetta. She may prove to be a challenge. At least Marie's a dear."

"That woman is wound as tight as my Bulova. She needs a man to help her relax," John said.

"Are you volunteering?" I asked. Lottie burst out laughing.

"Not me. I have my hands full with Rose."

I'd made up the story about the Chens, so we had a free couple of hours. We decided to drive around a bit and grab an early dinner before John and I checked into our hotel. We both needed to be back to Syracuse the next day.

We drove north to 58th Street and turned right toward Fifth Avenue.

Lottie pressed a finger against her window. "Oh, there's the site of the new Bergdorf's. Stop here."

We piled out of the car, stood on the sidewalk, and looked up at the imposing building.

Lottie launched into a spiel. "The Vanderbilt's mansion used to be here. Mr. Goodman picked the site and designed the building. Beaux-Arts style, although that's hard to see behind all that scaffolding. It should be up and running by Easter."

Lottie pointed up and to her right. "I'll be spending a lot of time there. On the sixth floor."

"With all the bigshots?" John asked.

"No. Down the hall from Gift Wrapping."

We studied the imposing building with its marble front and arched cutouts. It evoked a museum, a shrine to fashion rather than just another retail store.

"Very impressive," John said, "and right across from the Park."

Back in the Franklin we rode up Fifth Avenue along the east border of Central Park. Leafless trees permitted a clear view of the Park with its open spaces, massive rock formations, and serpentine paths. We passed two ponds and a large lake. We stopped around 96th Street, got out, and walked toward the lake.

"I had no idea that the Park was this huge," I said. "And smack dab in the middle of New York."

Huge it was. More than eight hundred acres of countryside over fifty blocks long. Like a human spine, it ran straight up the city's center, dividing it in two, the posh side to the east and the commonplace to the west. Although I did not know it then, it was be a place I would come to know nearly as well as Green Lake Park.

<u>January 14th, 45 Standard Street</u>

I'd finished my shift at the hotel, arrived home and picked up the day's mail from the front hall. I could tell that there was nothing from Lottie, whose distinctive stationery always carried traces of her favorite cologne.

I was missing her a lot. I'd traveled to the city twice to see her for long weekends, and she had come home once to see her parents (and me). We both knew that it wasn't enough, but I couldn't afford to turn down many more weekend gigs. The last thing I needed was to gain a reputation as an unreliable musician, one who fails to show up for jobs. In this business, dependability is everything; it even trumps talent. Plus, I needed the income if I was going to keep traveling back and forth from the City.

I sorted through the pile: a Sears catalogue; a couple of utility bills; a renewal notice from the musician's union. And a letter addressed in a familiar script. It was from Charley. I laid it on the kitchen table, unopened, with the rest of the mail.

I'll get to it when I get to it, I decided.

Chapter 18: Linger Awhile

<u>January 15th, 45 Standard Street</u>

After a good night's sleep and hearty breakfast of eggs and bacon, I had mustered the strength to tackle Charley's letter. I tore it open.

Dear Morey,

I am glad that you haven't thrown this letter in the trash. (Not that I would be surprised or blame you if you had.)

I have tried writing you several times, but ended up tossing out each attempt. Finally I decided that, despite how awkwardly I might convey my thoughts, it was more important that you heard them. Besides, you were always the one that was good with words.

From where you sit, I am betting that you think I have abandoned you. That I have settled into this big evil metropolis, had some luck in my career -- playing with top-notch bands and composing songs that, to my delight, get published and played. You probably also think that, now that I have been rubbing elbows with the big guys, I have cut the strings tying me to Syracuse. And to you.

Well, to be frank, it's partly true. Since moving here two years ago, I have grown to love this place; I think it's where I was meant to be. Remember all those times we listened to the records at Clarks Music and went back home, trying to recreate the tunes? Or when I read off the names of New York clubs in the latest issue of The Musical Courier and you would check out where they were on that dog-eared map of Manhattan? Or our talks about practicing to get good enough to move here and work? I'm living that now.

And work I have. My poor Paramount has had its strings replaced too many times to count and its drum has yellow streaks from the oil on my fingertips. I've even had to buy a second tuxedo because the cleaners down the street can't get it back to me in time for my next job. Adding in the rehearsals and my need to write some new numbers, I find very little time to sleep. (PLEASE DON'T LET FRANCES KNOW THIS.)

Sometimes I feel like an athlete training for the Olympics. While his coach lays out a rigorous schedule, the athlete goes beyond that, doubling his effort, because he wants to be the best in the world. He feels like crap, but decides that hard work and feeling like crap are a necessary part of success.

I know that I'm a lucky guy, and I realize that none of this would be possible without you.

I paused and reread the sentence, scarcely believing he had put that thought on paper.

After all, you gave me my first violin lessons and showed me the basics of composing. It was you who persuaded Frances to pay for those pricey lessons with Myron Levee and who lent me the money for the Iucci.

No, I haven't forgotten. And I know that I treated you, Joe, and Manny like drek that day, when you were only trying to help. I have thought about that a lot and have come to realize it was not about you or about Syracuse being a hick town (although it just might be). No. Maybe it was about me. About Charley Harris's insecurities. I think I was trying, in my bumbling way, to assure myself that I had graduated to the big leagues (even though I hadn't) and left my sleepy hometown behind.

Now that I have had some success and feel more secure, I'm no longer out to prove anything on that score. Instead I want to spend time with my only brother, and to show you what I have been up to here. And, just as important, to learn about what you have been up to there. (It would be so much better coming directly from you. I've had enough of our sister's jumbled version.)

So, I have a proposition. Take a few days off from the hotel, even bow out of a weekend gig and come to New York. I will take you around to some of my favorite clubs (some of the best music is up in Harlem). I should be able to find you a <u>paying</u> job sitting in with my band on Saturday. And, if after the week is up you can't stand being around me, we can go back to being brothers in name only, living our separate lives.

So big brother, the ball is in your court. You can dribble around all day in a circle or try to make a basket. It's your call.

Your loving brother,
Charley

<u>February 10th, 46 West 73rd Street</u>

I stopped by the super's office, picked up a key to Charley's apartment, and let myself in. Charley's letter had done the trick, and I was willing to give reconciliation a trial run.

The apartment was empty and still; the only sounds were the muffled noises from the street below. Charley was rehearsing with the George White Scandals Orchestra and wouldn't be back until dinnertime. I laid down my bag and violin case and began to explore the apartment. It was much as I'd remembered it -- Ross's grand piano at one end of the front room and bookcases at the other. Someone had hung a pair of handsomely framed drawings of musicians at work above the piano. In one, a pianist was seated, bent forward, hands on keys with his head turned toward the viewer as if he were playing for us. The other one was of a clarinetist, shown from the waist up -- instrument raised, eyes closed, and wailing out a tune.

I went into the kitchen and heated water for tea. Waiting to hear the kettle boil, I ventured into Charley's room. How neat it is, I thought, and so unlike the one we shared growing up. Several books were on the nightstand. To my surprise, none was about music. One was titled 'The Philosophy of Life'. It sat atop a book called 'Correct English', and nearby was a book called 'Etiquette'. All part of a recent quest for self-improvement, I guessed.

Then I noticed a stack of papers on his desk. Moving closer I realized that it was sheet music. I picked up the top one. Charley had written a title: Calling Satan, scratched it out and replaced it with Page Mr. Satan. A better choice. The piece was incomplete; he'd written only the first ten bars. Curious about how it would sound, I picked up the music, walked to the front room, opened my luggage, took out my fiddle and bow, and began playing. Like most of Charley's 'hot fiddling' numbers, this one had a fast tempo and was full of double stops, making it a challenge to play. But it had an original melody; I could imagine the Devil himself dancing along the strings.

Charley walked in at 6:00, looking haggard. Was it the hectic schedule he was keeping, lack of sleep, or something else, I wondered. He seemed genuinely happy to see me, his eyes tearing up a bit as we greeted each other.

"Dinner at Mr. Chen's. Is that o.k., Morey? Sweet and Sour?"

"Sounds perfect."

February 14th, Biltmore Theater

Ross and I were seated in the third row, anticipating a fine view of the performance. Charley was already on stage, first row, stage right, banjo in hand, and looking dapper in his tuxedo and shiny, just-purchased balmorals.

The orchestra began playing The Girl is You, and the Boy is Me. Lucky Day came next. Then the McCarthy Sisters joined the orchestra and sang a charming version of Tweet, Tweet. Tom Patricola, an up and coming young hoofer, did a rapid fire dance to Spanish Shawl. It may have been my imagination, but it seemed as though Patricola was timing his moves to Charley's playing more than to the rest of the orchestra, even glancing at him from time-to-time to synchronize their rhythms.

Any doubt I might have had that dancers liked my brother's playing evaporated with the next number. Ann Pennington was up. She was one of the Follies featured performers, the 'Black Bottom' girl. A tiny woman, only four feet ten inches tall and reputed to wear a size 1 ½ shoe, she was a larger than life performer who sang and danced with high energy. She favored lingerie-like costumes that underscored the seductive nature of her act.

Ann sang a spirited version of Black Bottom to the audience's delight, and then began to dance her signature number. The orchestra had been instructed to change key and to speed up the tempo. Unlike the usual group, this one, a blend of regulars and substitute musicians, had not rehearsed with her. After a few bars they became confused about the key change; some complied, while others stayed in the original key. The sound became muddled, like a junior high orchestra. Lost, the musicians anxiously look at each other.

Then Charley took charge. Playing his loudest, he picked up the tempo and slammed out the chorus. The other musicians stopped playing. Ann danced her rapid, seductive number to Charley's banjo solo, pausing in front of him suggesting that they were a team and that the impromptu duet had been planned.

After taking her bows, she slinked across the stage heading straight to Charley. She stopped, faced him, bent over and kissed him full on his lips while wriggling her rear end at the audience. Charley's face turned beet red. The crowd laughed, but I had a different reaction. While proud of his musical skill, I had a twinge of empathy for his vulnerability. All the musicians in the room, from the conductor to the second violinist, to Ross and me, realized that Charley had saved her number. Ann even insisted that their duet be repeated the following night. And so it was.

I never made it to Harlem that week, nor did I sit in with a big city band and get a big city paycheck. Yet the visit was a success; now I had my brother back.

Chapter 19: Side by Side

Landay Bros. Music, West 42nd Street

I stood near the entrance, poring through a stack of violin solos, in search of one I could work on back at the apartment. Clarks Music, Syracuse's premier shop and my favorite haunt, would fit in a corner of Landay's. Here I was in music heaven, and I did not want to leave.

"Come on, Morey. Let's get a move on," Charley called, closing the door behind him as he left a nearby listening booth, a Paul Whiteman recording in hand. Handing it to the clerk he turned to me, "We don't want to keep the girls waiting."

"Oh. Right. I just need to buy this Rubinoff piece."

Two months had passed since I had become Charley's roommate. Lou had packed up his trumpet and left New York for a band job in Chicago, freeing up a room in my brother's apartment. Happily, Ross and his baby grand remained, and Charley put it to good use, calling it his "composing partner".

Charley had persuaded me to move in, even found me a telegraph operator job, smoothing my move. What a difference a year makes. We had gone from not speaking to spending days together talking about everything, as if trying to catch up on lost time.

And now Lottie and I were not just in the same state, but the same city, three subway stops apart, making regular dating possible. Even Charley had benefitted from my move. Thanks to Lottie he found love. Her name was Marie Bradford; she was Lottie's roommate, the one Lottie had described as "a dear".

And a dear she proved to be. Marie entered my brother's life the very week I moved to the City. We had gone to Lottie's apartment Sunday morning to take her to breakfast. Marie was home and Lottie asked if she could join us. "Absolutely," Charley said after spotting Marie sitting on a couch. She was a knockout, a tall, slim raven-haired beauty who worked as a fashion model. Anything she put on looked chic, particularly when she used her runway walk, taking those smooth confident steps that showcased her and her outfits. On most women that gait would seem forced or odd, but somehow on Marie it worked. She was a fixture in magazine ads and a minor celebrity in fashion circles. Lottie had seen photos of her work before moving to the City and recognized her on sight.

Charley, who had no idea who she was, nevertheless, was smitten, and that breakfast marked a turning point in his life. With his looks and confidence, my brother had never been short of young women vying to spend time with him and had settled into a pattern of casual dates, fitted between jobs. For Charley weekends were for working, not playing around.

But change happens. Like Rip Van Winkle waking from his slumber, Charley came to life around Marie. As we'd walked along 54th Street that morning, Charley had peppered her with questions hoping to discover more about the attractive woman by his side. He learned that modeling was not something she had pursued, but that she had been 'discovered' by a photographer, that she liked modern music and was close to her family -- her parents and two siblings. (After they had been dating a few months, Marie's father, who owned a car dealership in Brooklyn, was so taken with Charley that he offered him a job in his business, an offer Charley would decline.)

Sugar Cane Club, 135th Street

Mamie Smith was onstage singing That Thing Called Love, her soulful voice -- part jazz, part blues -- drawing us into her world. Charley had discovered her at another club a few weeks earlier and insisted that we hear her. The singer was new to Lottie and Marie, and I had only heard her Okeh Records recording of Crazy Blues. I suspected that this was the first visit to Harlem for the girls. Charley and I had gone to Club Alabam' a few times, and heard some great music in a style different from the downtown clubs, less formal, more spirited, soulful.

Lottie was uneasy, seeming to like the performer ("She's good," she'd whispered in my ear), but not the venue. She sat upright in her chair, knees together, stiffly almost primly, an unnatural posture. From time to time she took dainty sips from her cocktail, stealing furtive glances around the room. I cupped my hand over hers, massaging her fingers slowly, in a vain attempt to help her relax. What was the problem, I wondered. Was it the audience, mostly colored? They were a far cry from her Fifth Avenue crowd. Or was it something else?

Marie was another story. Seated across the table from me, she looked as if she were sitting in her living room, relaxed, bent forward, wearing a half smile while soaking up every lyric. Her left pinkie tapped the rim of her Champagne glass to the beat of the music, while her right arm circled Charley's waist. From time to time she cocked her head sideways, resting it on his shoulder. Charley, wearing a wide grin, alternated between nursing his Old Fashioned and smoking his Pall Mall. Both seemed right at home, like regular denizens of this Harlem speakeasy.

46 West 73rd Street

The black bowtie hung on the room's door handle, Charley's version of a Do Not Disturb sign. He and Marie were in bed. Together. Again. She had become a regular visitor, often waiting outside our apartment for Charley to return from one of his band jobs and staying the night. They were hot for each other, their mutual attraction evident in their kissing, hand holding, hugging, and gazing that left Ross and me to wonder if they even realized we were there.

I was happy for Charley, but couldn't help to contrast their rabbits-in-heat dating style with Lottie's and mine. While attracted to each other, we were discrete, our public displays of affection being limited to hand holding and brief kisses. I never stayed the night at her apartment, nor she at mine. We still had a bit of the conservative Upstate mindset rattling around in our heads.

Chapter 20: S.S. Leviathan

"I'm curious," I said to Charley as we waited to cross Amsterdam Avenue on our way to the Chens. It was Tuesday and time for William's lesson.

"Curious is good. Gets the creative juices flowing."

"True, but I'm curious about something you did."

"Ah. The plot thickens."

"Well. You insisted that we take Lottie and Marie to The Sugar Cane, to hear Mamie Smith."

"Didn't you like her?"

"Oh, no, she was terrific, but it was an odd choice."

"How so?"

"Well," I said as we neared Mr. Chen's, "for the girls' first trip into Harlem, I would have picked a place like the Cotton Club."

"Where the colored musicians play to an all-white audience?" He shook his head, "Boring."

"Oh. Skip it….. But why Mamie Smith? The last I checked you were not a big fan of singers."

Charley stopped abruptly. He turned and faced me. "O.K. here's the scoop. You know Mamie's story, don't you?"

"Everyone knows about her Crazy Blues recording. It sold well."

"Well? A million copies the first year. But that's not what makes her special. She also dances and is a terrific piano player. She fought hard for that record.

Her producer even got death threats for recording a colored singer."

"She sounds ambitious."

"I'll say. She handpicked all her musicians, named her band 'Mamie Smith and Her Jazz Hounds,' firing many who didn't meet her standards. She became a kind of diva, toured Europe and went mainstream, even recorded for Victor. And guess what else?"

"I can't imagine."

"She's married to a landsman, Jack Goldberg."

"Wow. So you're a fan?"

"More than that. I want to emulate her."

"You mean marry a guy named Goldberg?"

"Such a comedian. No. My own band. Hire the players. Write the music. Record it and tour."

"Is that it? And all this time I thought you were ambitious."

Mr. Chen's Sweet and Sour, West 77th Street

We greeted the Chens and climbed the serpentine stairs to the apartment. William was waiting in the front, banjo in hand, obviously looking forward to the lesson. It had been quite a while since I'd seen him. The lean baby faced boy had filled out and matured, now a taller, beefier version of his father, but blessed with his mother's expressive eyes.

Charley asked William to play a piece he had been working on since the last lesson. After a few bars I realized it was Whiteman's Whispering. William's technique was fine, and he showed a feel for the music, but hadn't yet mastered the piece, stopping a few times to correct some wrong notes before moving on.

I watched Charley, his Paramount in hand, work with his student. He'd ask William to play a few bars and stop. Then Charley would play the same notes, talking it through. William would play the same section again, with Charley giving a running commentary. They continued this way through the whole piece. And it worked. Just over the course of that lesson William's playing improved.

Charley's fee was dinner, prepared by Mrs. and served by Mr. Chen. The couple had insisted I be their guest, even though I had done nothing to earn it. Another exceptional meal with enough leftovers for two more meals.

S.S. Leviathan, New York Harbor

Charley and I climbed the gangplank that led to the S.S. Leviathan, touted as the "World's Largest Ship". While I couldn't vouch for the accuracy of that claim, the ship was huge. It dwarfed us as we stepped aboard the steel behemoth, with too many levels to count topped by three gigantic, now dormant, smokestacks. In two days the ship would be leaving port for Southampton, England with Charley, among its thousands of passengers, on board.

He had taken a leave from Whiteman's orchestra to be a featured player with Kratke's Leviathan Orchestra. He was being paid top dollar and given a chance to see Europe -- albeit briefly, since the trip took five and a half days each way, and the ship left New York harbor every three weeks. It was mid-May, an ideal time to take the job, well past London's winter dampness. After all, cold weather and Charley never did get along.

Cruise Director Jack Harmon was on the main deck, surrounded by a half-dozen band members who were also there for the tour.

"We're standing on the main deck, a kind of common ground for passengers and crew. Anyone is welcome to use this space, unlike other parts of the ship."

For the next two hours we explored the ship, stem to stern, while Harmon led us around narrating the whole time. Neither Charley nor I had realized how stratified life on a cruise ship like the Leviathan would be. Even for paying passengers it was its own world with its own rules: who could be where and when; with privileges that could be given or held back based on what one had paid for the voyage.

At least Charley was luckier than most employees. He would be playing for First Class passengers, promising bigger tips than from other passengers. The First Class lounge was a large room furnished in miles of red velvet, mahogany furniture, and brass sconces all set beneath elaborate stained glass panels that covered the entire ceiling. A setting that could make even a mediocre band seem special. The program would be built around classical music and popular tunes, mainly dance numbers. Music easily mastered. Although not his favorite repertoire, the performance schedule was light, less than two hours of playing at night, leaving him free the rest of the time.

One look at his cramped living quarters, though -- six bunks in a modest room -- and we were reminded that he would be an employee, not a passenger. And the dining rooms were off limits; he would be taking his meals in the galley.

"So, you're off on a new adventure," I said.

"Yup. I get to see England and be paid to travel there."

"What does Marie think?"

"Don't know. Haven't told her. Yet."

Chapter 21: Whispering

Their voices rose and fell. A full-blown argument was underway.

"What do you MEAN,… didn't need ….. ME?"

"It's not my …job to…"

"So, that's wha…."

"Selfish….ard, you."

"Only three….MONTHS."

"So, you….. Think I ….care?"

"DAMN YOU."

Charley's door was closed, but there was no need for the Do Not Disturb bow tie. Nothing romantic was going on in that room. The last thing that Ross or I would have thought of was to interrupt them. We had been creeping around the apartment cat-like since the shouting started. Did Charley and Marie know we were there, just outside their door? Did they even care?

A loud sound shook the door, reverberating through the apartment. We flinched. Something had been thrown against it. Not his banjo, I hoped, more likely it was that thick "History of Classical Music" volume Charley kept in his bookcase.

A few gestures and whispers later Ross and I were on route to Landay's. The prospect of escaping to Whiteman or Bill Robertson in the privacy of a sound proof booth was too tempting to ignore.

The store was nearly empty, unusual for a Saturday morning. A clerk at the register, happy to see live customers, greeted us warmly, while a stock boy arranged sheet music in the store's Broadway Shows section. Ross made a bee line to the piano solos, and I headed to the big band records. I located a copy of Paul Whiteman's Whispering, found an empty booth, pulled the hefty shellac disc from its sleeve and settled in.

The lush sound of the orchestra's intro filled the booth, calming me. Then Jack Smith's rich tenor voice:

Whispering while you cuddle near me
Whispering so no one can hear me
Each little whisper seems to cheer me
I know it's true dear…there's no one dear but you.
Whispering why you'll never leave me
Whispering why you'll never grieve me
Whisper and say that you believe me
Whispering that I love you.

The raucous noise of the shouting match had faded, replaced by thoughts of Lottie and of how lucky I was to have her in my life. Unlike Charley and Marie, we never fought; ours was a calm, civil, even tempered relationship. We respected each other's feelings. I wouldn't dream of taking a job that kept us apart for weeks or months without asking her. But for my brother, career was paramount; everything else was secondary. To me relationships mattered most and my career could take a back seat. Maybe that was the main difference between us.

Two hours later Ross and I walked back to the apartment, wondering what we'd find. To my surprise the building was still standing and there were no bodies to be seen. We heard Charley humming along with his banjo to an unfamiliar tune. He was perched on his bed, calmly composing a new number, his bags packed and stacked neatly against the far wall. Marie was nowhere to be seen.

"Where did you guys go?" he asked, still strumming a tricky new chord.

"We stopped by Landay's," Ross answered.

"Thought you might need some privacy," I said.

"Oh. You mean our little tiff?"

I went into Charley's room and joined him on the edge of the bed. Ross discretely stayed in the front room, sat at the piano, and began playing some arpeggios.

"Charley," I began, "why did you wait until the eleventh hour to tell Marie about the Leviathan job?"

"Oh, I don't know." He paused the strumming, "I didn't need her permission to accept the gig."

"That's not the point."

"What do you mean?"

"Look. You're going to be away from each other for some time."

"Not that long. Plus she'll be here when I get back."

"And when will that be?"

"A few weeks, that's all."

The "few weeks" turned into the entire summer, as Charley ended up being rehired for two more rotations -

- three weeks traveling, one week back in New York and three weeks away. To his credit, Charley wrote Marie nearly every day. When she discovered that he wasn't writing me, she began stopping by the apartment every few days to share his letters.

Charley was in his element, writing about the prominent people he had met on the ship. Except for Al Jolson and Arthur Murray, most were unfamiliar to me. And then there were the London sights – Big Ben, The Tower of London, Westminster Abbey, and the Globe Theater. He described his visits to the Saville Row shops in Mayfair and his growing appreciation of bespoke tailoring. I had no idea what "bespoke" was, but Marie was happy to fill me in.

Ironically, I now saw Marie more often than I saw my own girlfriend. Lottie was busy working on the store's Fall line, so we spent only Sundays together. Near the end of one of her visits, Marie casually mentioned that a young fellow had been stopping by their apartment.

David Goldstein, Yetta's older cousin, was a medical student finishing his residency at Columbia. Initially he had come by to take Yetta to dinner, but recently, according to Marie, Lottie had been joining them.

"It's probably nothing, Morey, but I thought you should know."

"Hmm. Lottie's never mentioned him. What's he like?"

"Nice looking fellow. Good dresser. Pleasant personality, nothing like Yetta."

The following Sunday I asked Lottie about David. She seemed surprised that I knew about him, acknowledged that he "seems nice", and changed the subject.

Within a month it was over. Lottie had fallen for David, and he had fallen for her. Now I was history. After all, how could I, an itinerant musician and part time telegraph operator, hope to compete with a future physician? Although the "Syracuse Lottie" would not have sought out a doctor for a mate, the "Manhattan Lottie" would. She had changed since settling into the City, foreshadowed by her reaction that night at the Sugar Cane Club.

The Deutsches must be jumping for joy. And lucky Tova; he could now look forward to sniffing a new pair of feet, likely clad in Burberry wingtips.

Chapter 22: All Alone

Blindsided. The Lottie I had dated for more than a year, the one that I had moved to another city to be with, the one I had thought loved me was gone. In a heartbeat I went from boyfriend to no-friend. The girl I thought was mine had moved on, sped away as if driving one of John's Franklins, leaving me in the dust.

After all, wasn't I the attentive boyfriend who respected my sweetheart's feelings, never took her for granted? And where did it get me?

Meanwhile my callow brother, pursued by a beauty he treated with indifference, was never alone (except by choice). And he got to enjoy frequent, passionate lovemaking.

And then there was his career. Charley played with terrific bands, turning down more jobs than he could count. Other musicians, some with more years under their belt than he, went out of their way to hear him play because he was that good. And the pieces he composed were grabbed up by publishers, many ending up on the playlists of top notch bands.

After having played hundreds of blues numbers, I was now living one. As if I had lost a limb and was hobbling around. Directionless and depressed. In a funk, I spent my nights in the apartment. Alone. Everyone was gone; Ross was off playing a job in Chicago, while Charley was somewhere in the middle of the Atlantic. Arthur Murray and his partner were probably gliding across the ship's dance floor to Charley's rendition of Ain't We Got Fun.

The phone rang. It was Frances.

"Morey, why don't I ever hear from you?"

"I've been busy."

"Are you o.k.? You sound funny?"

"Well, Charley's off to Europe. Ross is away."

"And you broke up with Lottie."

"Actually, she broke up with me. How did you know?"

"Morey, dear Morey. Think."

"O.K. I'm thinking. So?"

"Syracuse is a small town, and Jewish Syracuse is even smaller. Every Jew knows what every other one is doing. Esther Klein told me the Deutches are giving an engagement party next month for Lottie and her intended. He's a doctor."

"Medical student. But close enough."

"I am sorry about it all. How are you holding up?"

"Frankly, I've been better."

For the next hour it was vintage Frances, working her magic. She got me to open up about the breakup, an event that I had thought was all Lottie's doing, unjustified, selfish, and cruel. She asked a few pointed questions about how I had been treating Lottie, what kind of attention I had (or had not) given her since moving here. Soon I began to realize that maybe I hadn't been as attentive as I'd told myself. My behavior could be seen as indifference, since my routine --

working two jobs and helping Charley with his composing -- often took precedence over Lottie, leaving her vulnerable to another man's overtures. Coupled with her understandable quest to adapt to the "Bergdorf Style", she was no longer the "Addis Girl" from Syracuse. In short, the breakup was on both of our heads.

Frances had also listened to my Charley-envy rant, calmly reminding me that ambition was Charley's thing, not mine.

"Morey, you have other qualities. You're not self-centered like Charley. You're considerate, kind even."

"I guess, but where will that get me?"

"Farther than you might think."

"Maybe."

"With Charley it's all about music. Period. End of story. But you're the one in our little family who excels in relationships. You don't intimidate people, so they're drawn to you. You've got more options."

The dark cloud was starting to lift.

She ended our phone marathon with news that she and Joe were hoping to celebrate their upcoming tenth wedding anniversary in Manhattan. They wanted to pick a weekend when both brothers would be in town. We settled on mid-October.

*****

The hostess showed the five of us to a table. Frances's outfit, well-tailored but not the latest style, contrasted with Marie's chic number. Charley looked dapper as usual in his double breasted suit and cap-toed shoes. The less said about Joe's outfit and mine, the better.

William and Mr. Chen arrived at our table, and Charley introduced Frances and Joe.

"Where Miss Lottie, this evening?" Mr. Chen asked.

William grimaced and I offered, "Damned if I know."

William whispered something in his father's ear. A pause. Then an "Oh, no."

Marie, who had been silently taking in the scene, put down her teacup and turned to Frances.

"So, what have you two been doing in New York?"

"Well. Last night we had dinner at the Ambassador and stayed to hear Charley play." Turning to Charley, "You sounded wonderful, by the way."

Turning back to Marie, "We even danced a bit."

"You danced, Joe?" I asked. "That must have been a first."

Frances cut me off. "Don't underestimate my husband. He's a really good dancer."

She paused and smiled. "For an accountant!"

"Well, I know how to count steps. And if I start and end with the music and haven't run into anybody on the floor, I consider it a success."

We laughed and began passing around the rice, shrimp and chicken dishes. We finished it all. No leftovers were taken home that night.

It was a special evening, one that I would remember fondly. Our family had been reunited, sharing a meal and memories in an adopted city.

We had no idea what was to come.

Chapter 23: Sidewalks of New York

1928 began on a high note. In January Norman Pierce, program director at WJZ phoned Charley at the apartment. After a long conversation, Charley hung up and announced that we had just been offered a job: Saturday afternoons, broadcasting, as the Hickville Hottentots, just violin and banjo. We'd have free rein with the only requirement being to finish up within our scheduled hour. A steady job that paid sixty dollars a month each, coupled with a potential audience of thousands. We accepted it without hesitation.

We had less than a week to plan our first broadcast. A steady menu of Charley's songs wouldn't work; it might turn off all but the diehard jazz fans. So we settled on offering a mix of familiar and new numbers. Dinah, My Blue Heaven, or The Sidewalks of New York might be followed by Charley's Bluein in Red or Rhapsodona.

Ever the promoter, Charley would introduce his own numbers: "This is Charley, and I wrote this next tune with a beautiful young lady in mind. As you listen, imagine her dressing for the evening, looking forward to a night of dancing with her beau." Vintage Charley, simultaneously promoting his work and making sure that the female listeners would remember his name.

And they did. After a few weeks the station began receiving fan mail, all from women. He showed some of it to me (but not to Marie). He found the letters more amusing than tempting; he would read them, smile, shake his head, and tear them up.

Soon we settled into our Saturday routine. We'd get to the station early, finalize the list of numbers and rehearse for a half hour or so. We would begin and end with popular numbers, hoping to hook the listeners at the start, and then later, leave them humming a familiar tune. Afterwards we'd stop by Bickford's for a late lunch, critique that week's show, and start to plan next week's.

For me these Saturday afternoons were the highpoint of the week. While the Monday through Friday work at the telegraph company paid the bills and I was good at it, it posed no challenge. I guess it was my musical background and inborn feel for rhythm -- after all dots and dashes are first cousins to notes and rests. I transmitted paragraphs of text rapidly and virtually error free, skills that did not go unnoticed by my supervisors. But there was nothing creative about the work. Indeed, "creative" tinkering with a message would get me fired fast. I was bound to a desk working seven hours at a stretch. Alone.

Saturdays were a whole other story. No longer an anonymous clerk, I had a new identity. I was a "Hickville Hottentot," a musician who offered any Manhattanite who tuned in to WJZ an hour of jazz, something a listener could tap his feet to, or even sing along with. What's more, I got to spend time with Charley, engaged in our favorite pastime -- making music.

The WJZ broadcasts reached another audience beyond lovelorn ladies -- musicians. From time to time they would call us at home or come up to us in a club and offer comments about the program. And every few weeks, or whenever we needed to round out the sound on a number, we'd have one of them sit in on piano or horn.

Whether it was the program's popularity, the incident with Ann Pennington when Charley saved her act, or something else, I will never know. But a week after his twenty-fourth birthday Charley was invited to interview for a dream job: music director for Meyer Davis's society orchestra. Joe Moss, Davis's senior manager, had called the house and invited Charley to Davis's office, asking that he bring along his banjo.

Unlike Whiteman, who was an innovative musician and composer, Davis was a conventional musician who managed a suite of orchestras. Charley was directed to meet Davis at the Waldorf-Astoria. The hotel's previous orchestra director had left and Davis was poised to take over. Davis was looking for a talented young musician to direct one of his society orchestras, one that would perform for private events across the City.

Later, Charley described their meeting.

Mr. Moss led Charley into the room and introduced him to Davis, whose impeccable dress and formal manner struck Charley as more fitting a banker than a musician.

"Morning, Mr. Harris. I've heard some good reports on your playing."

"I appreciate that, Mr. Davis."

"I see you remembered to bring along your instrument. Why don't you play something you wrote?"

Charley played a few bars of Rhapsodona to a poker faced Davis. He signaled Charley to stop and then asked him to play a few bars of Chinatown, stopped him again and asked for Linger Awhile.

"Not bad," he said, not looking at Charley but at the pad he was writing on.

"I don't want another banjo player or composer, but I do need a director. Someone who can manage some of my society work. He'd pick the numbers, rehearse them so they're perfect, and then conduct."

"Quite a challenge."

"Sure is. Are up to the job?"

"Yes, I believe I am. It's something I've been preparing for."

"I see." Davis took a hard look at Charley. "How old are you?"

"Twenty-four, sir."

"That's young. Some of the older guys will resent you telling them what to do."

"I've already encountered that challenge, sir. With my SS Leviathan Orchestra. At first they were wary, but they came around soon enough."

Finally showing some reaction, Davis laughed. "Cocky and talented."

He stood, signaling that the interview was over. Turning to his right he said: "Mr. Moss here will prepare a contract. Can you start on the twenty-sixth?"

Mamie Smith and the Sugar Cane Club, that's what came to my mind when I heard the story. Less than a year had passed since that Harlem visit and, taking a page from the diva's career, Charley was on his way to adding two more notches to his musician belt. Next to "performer" and "composer" he'd carve "manager" and "conductor". And for one of Manhattan's premier orchestras.

He plunged headlong into the job, as if little else mattered beyond proving that Meyer Davis had chosen well. We kept the WJZ gig, but now I took the lead on that, picking the play lists and rehearsing -- some weeks, alone. To be fair, Charley's new assignment was daunting, and even he was surprised at its scope. He not only had to find, secure, and tailor the song selections to the season and the audience, rehearse and conduct the music, but also pick the players. Some of the band members in the Davis stable failed to meet my brother's high standards. He would recommend that they be let go and, if approved, would cast about for stronger players to replace them.

This frenetic pace took its toll. Already slim, Charley lost weight and looked haggard. Concerned with his health, Marie had insisted he eat regular meals, preferably with her so she could monitor them. At first Charley resisted, but in the end, he grudgingly complied. The tension over his eating did not affect their love life, however. The bow tie made regular appearances on Charley's doorknob, to the envy of Ross and me.

With my own brother managing a first rate orchestra, I harbored some hope that the Davis organization might consider taking me on. After all I reasoned, my fiddling was as good as most of the other string men, and I could use the work. I never asked Charley, though, and it never happened. Maybe it shouldn't have. If he'd hired me, or persuaded Davis to take me on, I would be in my kid brother's employ, and we would cease being equals. Lord knows where that might have led.

As busy as Charley was, we still found time to enjoy the City. Together. New York had much to offer beyond music -- the City Planetarium, ball games, and Coney Island rides. We sandwiched them in between jobs, sometimes accompanied by Marie. A generous spirit, she didn't object to my tagging along on some of their dates.

But music, including Broadway musicals, was our favorite diversion. One night we took in Hoboken Blues at the New Playwrights Theater, a show that we both liked for its innovative musical numbers. Unfortunately, it had a short run (thirty-five performances), so by the time Charley wanted to return with Marie, it had closed.

Short runs were not a problem for the George White's Scandals. They appeared and reappeared over the decade, changing songs and performers, but always using the same format -- musical numbers strung together with a thin story line. Somehow they worked. The 1928 version featured Tom Patricola and Ann Pennington, two stars that Charley had kept in touch with since the Biltmore Theater incident when Charley

145

had saved the day. Tom had gotten the three of us tickets to a show that introduced a new performer, Boots Mallory. She was a stunner, a tall, blue eyed blonde who sang and danced up a storm, although from where I sat she could have just stood still on stage and I would have been happy.

To my delight, Tom and Ann invited us to go to dinner after the show, and Boots joined us later. Seeing Ann and Boots side by side was striking. Although both were beauties, with Ann at four feet, eleven and Boots at five feet, nine, they appeared to be from two separate species. A point that they readily and happily acknowledged, referring to themselves as "the twins".

As I think back on it, I realize that Manhattan was the force that reunited the two of us. The ties that had frayed were mended. It was as if Charley and I were back at our boyhood home in Syracuse, sharing a room, and imagining our future.

Chapter 24: Is Everybody Happy?

Manhattan was thawing. Subtle signs of spring appeared quietly, like hushed whispers. Not yet budding, branches on Central Park's elms thickened, their sap beginning to run. People walking by our window still wore their winter coats, but had abandoned gloves, scarves, and hats, and their pace had relaxed as they no longer scurried to seek the comfort of a warm building.

A new season, a time for taking stock. Nearing thirty, and with my music career at a standstill, I wondered if I was on the right path. I had a gig most weekends and enjoyed playing with bands around the City, butI was stuck in the middle of the pack, earning more as a telegraph operator than as a musician. Plus my playing jobs weren't steady; I had yet to land a long term contract with an orchestra anywhere in the City.

Then there was my social life. After Lottie and I called it quits, I had had my share of dates. Thanks to Marie some were models, others were girls I had met through my band jobs, and one was a secretary at the telegraph company. They were an attractive, personable group and I had had some good times, but I never connected with any of them the way I had with Lottie.

And I was haunted by the thought that as a struggling musician, I had lost out to a future doctor. A medical career was not in my future, but another profession could be.

In early April I was back in Syracuse -- for a visit. It was Passover and Frances had invited Charley and me to her Seder. Charley declined. The Davis job had expanded, and he was now coordinating the performances in New England too -- not an assignment he'd have picked. He'd thrived on what he called 'Manhattan energy'. Once, on returning from a gig in Providence, he said: "That city, if you can call it one, is so dead. I could have shot a cannon down the main street at noon and not hit a thing."

Thus I came to Syracuse alone. The holiday ritual, the familiar food, and the town's leisurely pace had a calming effect. Soon my Manhattan-induced tensions evaporated. Two nights after the Seder, I dropped by the Valley Inn and sat in with Pop Barnard's group. Now I was back making music Syracuse-style, standard pieces played with enthusiasm rather than perfection, to an appreciative audience.

The next morning the doorbell rang. John Wilkinson's towering frame filled the doorway.

"Morey, I heard you were back in town. Come along with me. For a little ride."

And a 'little ride' it was. Four short blocks, down Waverly Avenue's steep drop to the eastern edge of the university campus. We could have walked it with ease, but I suspected John wanted to show off his latest Franklin (a green sedan with a brown interior). We parked near Steele Hall, and a few minutes later were sitting across from Dr. Simpkins, the same professor whose lecture I had sat through a year earlier.

"I remember this fellow," he said to John. "He's the note taker from a while back."

Simpkins looked as beefy as I had remembered him, but now his suit fit and his white shirt was freshly pressed. His wife's doing, I guessed. And chalk dust was nowhere to be seen.

Bewildered, I turned to John: "So. Why am I here?"

Before he could answer, Professor Simpkins spoke up. "It's John's doing. He's responding to my announcement of a new initiative here at SU. We're looking for ways to attract older students into our ranks by offering scholarships to strong applicants."

"Why would that interest me?"

It was John who answered: "Why not? Morey, we both know that the music business is very competitive and unstable. Long term you need a real profession. Like engineering."

Turning to Simpkins he launched into a sort of sales pitch. "Morey is one of the smartest fellows I know. He graduated at the top of his class at Central. High grades in math and science. A natural for engineering."

Simpkins looked at me with a 'So what do you think, young man?' expression. John's look signaled 'I have just revealed some profound truth that just might change your life, buddy.'

149

"Morey," Simpkins offered, "why don't you take some time to think about it. Applications aren't due for another month."

*****

I was seated on Frances and Joe's back porch poring over Chapter 3 in 'An Introduction to Mechanical Engineering' -- underlining passages. Writing notes in the margins. The Wilkinson-Simpkins tag team had won out, persuading me to start studying engineering. I had applied for admission that May and a few weeks later learned I had been accepted to SU's Engineering School, Class of 1932.

I had left Manhattan. Not an easy decision. It meant quitting my telegraph operator job and the radio show; I would miss the latter, but not the former. When I shared my plans, most guys in my circle thought it a savvy decision, one that could open doors music wouldn't. The Chens, including William, were at once surprised and happy that I was going to college. When I told them, Mrs. Chen hugged me, her eyes tearing as she said: "When you graduate, make us nice new building. We open restaurant there."

Charley was not surprised about my plans. Years before he too had suggested I think about college, since I had been 'the smart brother'. He said he'd miss rooming and working together, but, in reality, his chaotic travel schedule meant he was rarely in the City for more than a few days a month.

Frances, of course, was euphoric at the prospect of having a brother pursuing a degree and living in the same town. "You can have the spare room. No charge. And you can get to classes in a flash."

"Very generous offer, Sis. I'll try it out for the first semester. Until I settle in."

Soon I was into a new routine, one dramatically different from my Manhattan life. In place of living with two fellows and working nine to five, I was now nested in a household with two adults and three young children. We settled into our respective work week rhythms -- Joe off to his office, Frances to temple meetings, and the girls to school. I had classes three days a week, studied on the other days, and played jobs around town on weekends.

The girls seemed to enjoy having "Uncle Morey" around, especially when I entertained them with my fiddle and my not-too-scary ghost stories. Shirley, now eight and a music fan, was especially curious about my violin, and soon I was giving her lessons, much to Joe and Frances's delight.

Then there were my classes: Physics I, General Chemistry, Calculus and Mechanical Engineering, each with its own challenges, but none that I couldn't meet, evidenced by the A's and B's I earned. Initially I had harbored doubts about school. After all I had not been in a classroom in more than a decade, putting me at a disadvantage to my younger classmates. But soon I settled in, finding myself comfortable with the material. Perhaps the skills developed in my music --hours of practice, the quest for perfection, and the need to memorize tunes -- helped counter the time away from the tasks of solving equations and calculating strengths of material.

The move from telegraph operator to student was only one change. Another was from fiddle player to clarinetist. Back in New York, when Charley had been away on tour and I needed to occupy my time, I had retrieved my old clarinet and refined my rusty skills. After a bit, real notes replaced squeaks and screeches and recognizable melodies appeared. Not yet confident enough to play in public, I had stuck with the violin. But my new schedule freed up more practice time and my playing improved. At last I was ready to make my debut.

I even had a routine in mind to accompany my renewed skill -- impersonating Ted Lewis. Lewis, an iconic figure in the Manhattan music scene, was one of Columbia Records top recording artists. Dressed in a tuxedo, wearing a battered top hat, and alternating between his clarinet and singing, he was the consummate showman. Like Mamie Smith, Lewis had a band populated with some of the City's best musicians. Charley and I had gone to hear him at Reisenweber's Café.

Lewis began his show with his signature opening, "Is everybody happy?" Charley and I joined the crowd with the "Yes, we are!" response he always received. Lewis was a trouper, his packed show included renditions of Frankie and Johnnie, Just a Gigolo, When My Baby Smiles and Me, and a dozen others. His style was unique, superb clarinet playing interspersed with talking through, rather than singing, the numbers.

(Years later Jimmy Durante would copy Lewis's style with similar success.)

As we were leaving the theater, Charley turned to me and said, "You know, Morey, he reminds me of you."

"You're kidding."

"Yes. He does. Same eyes. Same expression and neither of you can sing worth a damn."

"Should I be thanking or cursing you?"

"No. Seriously. If you perfected the clarinet and picked up a tux and top hat, you could be his stand in."

Two years later, it's Saturday night, and I'm on stage at the Dew Drop Inn, doing my best Ted Lewis imitation, asking "Is everybody happy?" Like Ted's crowd back at Reisenweber's Café, I was hearing a chorus of "Yes, we are!"

And so was I.

Chapter 25: Birth of the Blues

It started with a cough. Probably a simple cold, Charley thought. New York had taken on that damp chill that accompanies fall in the North, a hint of the cold weather to come. He dreaded winter-- the fewer hours of daylight meant sunless streets would greet him in the early morning when he headed home from a gig. He'd have to wear layers of clothing in a quest to keep warm. The snow that began life white and airy would soon turned black and dense, unsightly and hard to navigate.

Most years, a cough and the fall would arrive together. His lungs were never strong, probably a result of inhaling the thick smoke during our house fire decades ago. The hacking -- sometimes intermittent like the striking cymbal in Bizet's Carmen, other times rhythmical, like the downbeat of Strauss's Blue Danube -- greeted Charley nearly every November. He'd nurse it for a week or two -- hot tea, rest, an aspirin every few hours -- and then it would be gone.

This time it was different. Like an annoying houseguest that had overstayed his welcome, the cough lingered. For the first week it was a simple distraction; he needed to wait it out just as he had done in the past. But when the second week arrived, it became more insistent, Bizet's cymbals crashed day and night. On the third week the night sweats began soaking his bedsheets. Food, even Mr. Chen's Orange Chicken, had lost its taste. He knew something was very wrong, but he said nothing. Even to Marie.

He couldn't afford to be sick and jeopardize his budding career. He was just settling into a new job. He had left Meyer Davis's outfit for a better arrangement with Jackie Taylor's, managing his society work in the Southeast. The Carolinas, Georgia, and Florida were perfect places to spend the winter. If he had stayed with Davis, he would be heading for cold New England and banking a smaller paycheck. A new job. New possibilities.

If only he felt better.

I didn't know about all this, of course, until later. I was working through a thermodynamics problem on my slide rule when the call came. I had moved out of Frances and Joe's to an apartment on Roosevelt Avenue not far from campus. The rent was low, and I had my privacy.

At first I couldn't understand who was calling. Marie's clear, lilting voice was replaced by a stranger's quavering wail.

"Charley's sick."

"My God. What's wrong with him?"

"He's coughing nonstop," she said, struggling to get out the words. "Won't eat anything… And is burning up. Come down here. Please."

"Of course. Call a doctor; I'll be there tomorrow."

The cough from Charley's room greeted me as I dropped my bag, a wrenching, full throated sound, audible even through the closed door. Marie greeted me, but sat motionless on the couch.

"Thanks for coming, Morey." Nodding her head toward Charley's room, she added, "David's examining him now."

I joined her on the couch and we sat silently. I looked around the room. Little had changed since I had lived there -- same couch and chairs, same stack of books, same piano still dominating the room. Yet everything was different. The light filled and vibrant apartment I remembered now seemed dark and heavy. Once a familiar landscape, now a foreign land.

Charley's door opened. "You can come in now," said a voice from Charley's room.

I caught my breath and willed myself to approach the bedroom. Entering, I saw the broad back of a young man, stethoscope in hand, one end resting on Charley's chest. He appeared to be asking Charley questions, but his voice was so low I could not make out the words. I walked to the bed. Charley was bone thin, his skin gray and his breathing labored. The contrast between this hale physician and my frail brother was unnerving. It was as if the doctor could fold his wisp of a patient in thirds, like a letter, stuff him into an oversized envelope, and carry him, one-handed, out of the apartment.

I greeted Charley, who in a hoarse voice between coughs, introduced me to David Goldstein, a fourth-year medical student at Columbia. Marie had called him and, respecting Charley's reluctance to go to a hospital, asked him to see Charley. Apparently he had done a thorough exam, judging from the copious notes laying on the bed beside him.

David Goldstein was Lottie's fiancé.

The man who had stolen my girlfriend was working to save my brother.

David finished his exam and gestured for Marie and me to go back to the front room. Gingerly, he closed Charley's door.

"I won't beat around the bush," he said in a measured tone. Turning first to me, and then to Marie, he added, "Charley is very ill."

Marie lowered her head and sunk into the sofa, her whole body limp.

He continued. "He told me he hadn't seen anyone about these symptoms."

"He just returned from Florida," Marie whispered. "I came by, saw that he was ill. Called Morey and you right away."

"I knew about that nasty cough. I heard it over the phone and urged him to have it looked at," I said, "but he said that the Florida sun would fix him up."

"I'm afraid we're well beyond that point," David said. "I'm going to call an ambulance. We need to get him over to Columbia and run some tests."

"What do you think he has?" I asked.

"Well, it's definitely respiratory. Could be any number of diseases, and I don't want to speculate. My supervisor is a pulmonary specialist. I'll ask him to examine Charley."

The next day we knew. Charley had tuberculosis. That terrifying disease that claimed half of its victims had attacked my dear brother. Devastating news. There was only a fifty-fifty chance I'd continue to have him in my life.

Willing myself to calm down, I gathered my strength and called Frances.

"Why are you in New York?" she asked.

I told her the bad news. A gasp. Then a long silence.

"Are you still there?"

"Yes," she finally said. "I was thinking. I want you to bring Charley home….. To Syracuse."

"But Manhattan has the best hospitals. He'll get the latest treatments here."

"Maybe. But the sanatorium is just down the road. It has a wonderful reputation. And we can visit him often. Make sure he's getting the proper care."

Ten days later Charley was admitted to the Onondaga Sanatorium, becoming one of two hundred forty patients hoping to stave off death.

Opened in 1916, the Onondaga Sanatorium was built in response to the tuberculosis epidemic that had been spreading for a decade. Frances was right, it was among the best, most advanced facilities in the State. Originally able to accommodate only one hundred patients, its capacity was expanded dramatically the year Charley was admitted. Superintendent Harry Brayton implemented an aggressive treatment regime combining heliotherapy that employed artificial light and sunshine treatment, with drug, nutritional and occupational therapies.

A resident physician met with us and confirmed our fear that Charley had an advanced case of the disease, but assured us that they were hopeful he would improve. Though we almost lost him the first month, by the second he seemed to rally. His cough subsided, he regained some of his lost weight and became more animated.

During one of our too-brief visits (by house rule, they were limited to thirty minutes), Charley asked me to retrieve a box that he had stored under his bed. The box, along with his banjo, was one of the few items he had brought with him from the City. I laid it on the bed. He took out a thick folder, labeled Rhapsodona, and opened it.

Charley had already worked out the motif, melodies and instrumentation for the three main characters -- the noblewoman, her lover, and her husband. The first section, about the noblewoman, was the piece he had published and played with Rudy Vallee. The other two were yet to be written.

He walked me through his notes and score sheets. He imagined a long piece, fully orchestrated with musical themes that would first be separate, then interweave, and separate once again. The noblewoman's theme was written for the violin. The lover would be carried by a piano, and the husband by a clarinet. Ambitious and original, it would be Charley's Rhapsody in Blue.

Work on the composition became a sort of therapy. He would sit in the light filled day room writing down his ideas. Once I brought my violin and played a section for him. When I finished we heard some applause from across the room. Charley cracked a smile, the first one I had seen since he entered the facility.

Too soon the smile faded. In February, Charley contracted an infection, one that his weakened immune system could not fight.

On March 4, 1929, Charley died at twenty-five. A life interrupted, two-thirds unlived. Rhapsodona was still unfinished and dozens more compositions unwritten.

For me, time itself had stopped. It was as if the first of three reels of a running movie had jammed. Try as he might, the projectionist could neither restart nor remove the reel. Confused, the audience sat silently as the white blob in the screen's upper right corner grew, obliterating the image and consuming it in a bright white light.

No one would ever know how the story turned out.

Chapter 26: After You're Gone

"We can't say *tuberculosis*," Frances shouted, her normally soft voice absent. "People will think Charley was some sort of vagabond. Or worse, a lowlife."

"But that's what killed him," I said. "We should be honest."

"What for? We have to think of our reputation."

"So what do you suggest?"

Frances paused, thinking. "Fatal illness. That's it. 'Charles Saul Harris died after a fatal illness.' If you have to be more specific say 'throat ailment'."

And so I did. I wrote Charley's obituary (with Frances's edit) and sent it to two New York City papers along with the Syracuse Herald and the Orchestra World.

Here is the Orchestra World version:

Charles Saul Harris

The sad death of Charles Saul Harris, one of the most promising of the music world's young musicians and composers, occurred recently. Charles was born 25 years ago in Plattsburg. On coming to New York he began his career with Benny and Carl Fenton. He worked with Paul Whiteman at Waymore in Atlantic City and later directed all of Meyer-Davis's society work. His fatal illness began in Florida, where he was

161

working with Jackie Taylor. On his return from the South he was with the Ipana Troubadours and Ernie Golden, besides playing, as in previous summers, with the S.S. Leviathan Orchestra.

Charles was the composer of the first "hot fiddle" solos which appeared on the market. Among his numerous compositions, "Hot Strings", "Hickville Hot", "Some Fiddling", "Rhapsodona", "Bluin' in Red", "Bowin' in Blue", "Page Mr. Satan", were particularly well known.

Charles was also the leader of the Hickville Hottentots which had been broadcasting over WJZ regularly. His untimely death was a blow to the metropolitan orchestra circles, where he is mourned by a host of friends and associates.

Keeping with tradition, temple volunteers washed, prepared Charley's body, and placed it in a pine coffin that now sat in Frances and Joe's living room. Against the same wall that had held Mimi's birthday party "Pin the Tail on the Donkey" game. She and her sisters were staying down the street at a neighbor's.

We had agreed to abide by most of the rituals -- sitting Shiva for seven days, draping mirrors, arranging for handwashing, and providing a continuous stream of food for visitors. Wisely, we drew the line at not bathing for the week.

The crowd, almost too large to count, filled the living room, spilling into the dining room and hallway. Family, friends, high school buddies and local musicians who had played with Charley and me stood shoulder to shoulder to the Manhattan crowd -- friends and musicians who had worked with Charley: William Chen; roommates Lou and Ross; Ferde Grofe; Benny Fenton; Jackie Taylor; and Henri Klickmann, Charley's arranger. Marie, visibly distraught, was accompanied by Lottie.

Benjamin Stoltz, Temple Concord's president, stood next to Charley's coffin and led the service. I struggled through a brief eulogy, then William and I played a mournful rendition of Rhapsodona as a banjo - violin duet.

We caravanned the short distance to the Chevra Chas Cemetery on Jamesville Road where Charley's body was laid to rest, only yards from our mother's plot. Standing by the graveside it struck me that Charley was probably one of the cemetery's youngest residents.

It was the evening of a very long day, the kind you think will never end. The house was still full of visitors chatting and dining, but I needed to be alone. Hoping some fresh air might revive me, even lift my mood, I put on my boots and coat and called to Joe that I was going for a walk.

The brisk night air greeted me as I stepped onto Frances and Joe's porch, and my head began to clear. I descended the steps and walked east, crossed Ostrom Avenue, stepping cautiously around the street's shimmering ice patches. Stone steps led me into Thornden Park and onto a level lawn. The sound of grass under my boots took on a regular rhythm. Ker-Crunch. Ker-Crunch. Ker-Crunch. The winter was winding down. Pillows of white appeared here and there, but much of the ground was the brown-green of grass gone dormant.

I walked deep into the park, past the straw covered rose garden, the iced-over frog pond, and the now still waterfall. Leaving the grass, I stepped onto the road and began to climb the serpentine route that led to the park's peak. The grand gas lamps that bordered the park and the lights from the neighboring houses glowed. Scattered jewels piercing the darkness. I climbed further. The stone clubhouse and ball field, framed by the white pines their branches outstretched like arms, faded in the distance. A handful of skaters, now barely visible, glided across the rough-hewn oval rink by the clubhouse.

I reached the top, out of breath, and sat on a nearby bench, its cold iron slats that had been painted long ago were now peeled and rusted. I breathed in deeply, the frigid air cut my lungs like tiny shards of ice.

I looked around. The park's water tower loomed to my left, its massive size dwarfing me. A water filled steel drum built for a disaster that would never happen, I thought. Unlike the one I am living through now.

As I sat, consumed by grief, I looked up, expecting a light filled sky, but saw only a scattering of stars. And the moon was a mere comma of light, a single white eyelash painted in bold relief against a coal black canvas.

Chapter 27: In a Mist

The syncopated strains of Bix Beiderbecke's In a Mist filled the apartment. I never tired of hearing the recording with its repeating da dum dum refrain and variations. Beiderbecke's clever riffs and breaks, and the way his fingers traveled around the keyboard, drew me in. It was like a refined version of honky-tonk. And it made me smile.

I was in a reflective mood. A year had passed since Charley's death, and so much had happened. None of it good. The stock market had crashed and times were tough. Decent jobs all but evaporated and people had lots of free time, but little money to do much with it.

I was better off than many. With no family to support, I only had to worry about Morey. My classes kept me busy and, thanks to support by the city, I still had regular gigs and some income. But the halcyon times that Charley and I shared were gone and not likely to return any time soon. Maybe never.

By the twelfth bar, Beiderbecke's fingers were flying. His rendition reminded me of Charley's banjo fingering -- fearless, confident, and technically flawless. A kind of muscular approach to the music. So different from my more measured playing.

When the song ended I placed the needle carefully back at the beginning and stretched out on the sofa. As I listened to those opening notes again, my mind drifted to a picture of what a Charley-less future might be.

"More chicken, dear?"

"Yes. Thanks," I answer, as my wife hands me a steaming bowl of chop suey.

Bathing in the glow of the overhead chandelier, our party circles a large table in the restaurant's back corner. The sweet aroma of just-served dishes swirls around us, lending a festive air. We had come to Mr. Chen's to celebrate William's performance at the Perroquet in Greenwich Village. Accompanied by Lou and Ross, he had played a mix of contemporary and classic pieces, most on banjo, a few on violin. The Times would later laud their performance as "engaging" singling out William as "...demonstrating equal mastery of two instruments" and as "the City's first world-class Oriental jazzman."

Frances and Joe sit to my left. While Joe talks baseball with Marie's husband, Frances is silent, carefully spooning rice from a serving bowl to her plate. She seems distant, lost in her thoughts, probably of Charley. More than seven years have passed and, more than anyone, Frances has yet to come to terms with his death.

As the meal winds down William stands and clinks a chopstick against his water glass:

"Thank you all for coming to hear us perform tonight." Looking at Lou and Ross he continues. "We had a great time putting the program together and we're pleased with how it went."

Lou and Ross nod.

"But I want to give a special thanks to the man who made it all possible. Charley Harris started me on this path, inviting me into the world of jazz and giving me the confidence to master an instrument. His joy for music, for the banjo, and for composing was infectious, and I am proud to say that I was his student. So thank you, Charley."

Almost in unison we lift our glasses and say, "To Charley."

We finish our meal and begin our goodbyes. As I walk toward the door I notice something new -- a series of photos along a wall. I pause and look; they depict celebrities who have dined here -- Arthur Murray, Paul Whiteman, Babe Ruth, Jack Dempsey, Louise Brooks, and others.

Then I see it -- an 8 by 10 photo of Charley in a black wood frame -- the light from a nearby Chinese lantern reflected in its glass. Charley is sitting, dressed in a tuxedo, and holding his banjo. His face is in profile and he is looking at the Paramount. A novel pose, one that suggests an unspoken connection between a musician and his instrument.

I look closer. In the bottom right corner, in that same overly adorned script he had first used as a high schooler, he had written:

To the Chens, My Manhattan Family.
Yours fondly,
Charles Saul Harris

I call everyone over, and one-by-one we examine the photo and murmur approving comments. As if from nowhere a young man appears, holding a camera. He directs us to gather around the photo and to form two row -- Frances, Marie, Mr. Chen, Mrs. Chen, and my wife in front, and Ross, Lou, Joe, William, Marie's husband and me in the rear.

A bright flash capturing a tableau: eleven of us flanking a photo and celebrating music in a restaurant on Manhattan's Upper West Side in the summer of 1936.

The hissing sound of a needle spiraling toward the center of the disk ended my reverie. I walked across the room, replaced the arm in its cradle, turned off the phonograph and retrieved my physics notebook. Music and the future would have to wait. I had an exam to study for.

Chapter 28: Coda
Mr. Paramount

Arlington, VA: 2015

A loud crash wakes me. "Shit, that hurts," a man says. "Damn box." I hear him hopping on one foot, muttering and cursing.

It's very cold and there's a musty smell. The man lifts and carries me. A clumsy carry. I hear a door open, then close. He lowers me onto a surface and undoes the buckles on my case. Snap. Snap. I hear the zipper on the lining open. A bright light blinds me. Unfamiliar hands lift me from my coffin.

The man speaks. "Let's get a good look at you."

He twirls me around in his hands. "I'd forgotten what a beauty you are."

New York City: 1927

Man No. 1, "What a beauty. Is that a Paramount?"

Man No. 2, "Yup, the Leader Special. I bought it a few weeks ago."

"How do you like it?"

"Well, it looks great, but I'm not crazy about the sound. Awfully tinny."

"Can I try it?"

I am handed to Man No. 2. He studies me, twisting me in his hands. Slowly. Carefully. He looks at my head, heel, and neck. He peers at my brass pieces, tension hoops, tone rings and flanges. I think they're my best features. Then he flips me around and studies my heel.

"Nice inlay work," he remarks as he starts strumming my strings. The fingers on his left hand dance up and down my frets. He tightens the peg on my A string. Begins playing an unfamiliar tune. His touch is assured, a skilled musician. His fingers fly across my strings. I think I've never sounded so good.

After a bit he says, "I've been thinking of replacing this Iucci. Moving up a few notches. This would fit the bill."

"I might sell it if the price is right."

"What if we trade? My banjo plus one hundred dollars for yours?"

"Let me try your Iucci."

He plays a few bars. Nods his head. They shake hands, and the deal is done.

My new owner swaddles me in my case and takes me home.

Soon Charley and I are inseparable, making music together. Sometimes it's just the two of us. I like the carefree way Charley plays when there's no audience. Other times we're with my friends -- saxophone, drum, trumpet, and trombone. My favorites, though, are violin and guitar; those of us with strings have a special bond. I like it best when there's no piano. I can't believe we're in the same family. Such a pompous one. He never moves; everyone has to come to him. So large, acting like he owns the stage. And all those strings.

Why does he need them? I make music with only four. Then there's his fancy keys. Shiny, white and grinning, like a phony smile with pieces of licorice between his teeth.

Charley always sits in front. I am on his lap, leaning to the left. The other players sit nearby. I like the solos, when we get to show off. We look out and see the audience listening, nodding their heads in time to our rhythm. When we finish, people applaud. Sometimes they dance. I like to see them move around the floor to our rhythm. We make them happy.

We practice every day. I like our practice time. Charley goes over a phrase. Stops. Thinks a bit. Plays it again. Changing it each time. Faster. Slower. Louder. Softer. After a while he strings the phrases together. Over the weeks I have felt the skin on his fingertips growing thick. Hours go by, but he never seems to tire. He stands, puts me down and shakes his arms while making a strange 'Mmmm' sound. He picks me up, and we start again.

In the morning he writes. He begins by striking a chord on me, hums a melody, stops and jots down the notes on manuscript paper. He continues until the chorus is finished. Then he moves to the middle strains, from the 17th to the 24th measures. Later, he revisits the melody, reworks it. Finished with the draft of a number, we play it all the way through. His facial expressions tell me what parts he likes and which ones he doesn't. He has a code -- pluses, minuses, checks and circles -- that he enters on the sheet on the table next to us. These marks remind him which sections were o.k. and which he needs to work on later.

Sometimes we are joined by Morey, his brother, and Morey's violin. The four of us play Charley's music and other songs. My favorites are Rhapsodona and Hot Strings. I also like Page Mr. Satan. We start out in unison; Charley and I are in the lead, Morey and violin accompany us. On the next number we switch. We sound good together. The two brothers like each other; they make jokes. They laugh together. I am lucky.

As Morey leaves he turns to Charley, "See you soon, kid."

Syracuse, NY: 1929

"Well kid, we're on," Morey says to me as he turns around and looks over the room. It is filled with people. No one speaks. I am held by strange hands. Morey and his violin stand nearby. Where is Charley?

Morey turns to the crowd. "Charley lived for music, to hear it, to play it and to write it. William Chen, one of my brother's students, and I will play Charley's composition, Rhapsodona. It's a number he wrote soon after moving to New York. It has been performed by many bands around the City."

We begin paying. The tempo is slower than when Charley and I played. William's fingers are less sure than Charley's, as if he is still learning the tune. Morey and his violin carry us along. We finish. There is no applause. Only silence.

Morey speaks again, "Charley Harris was a 'musical prodigy'. As a young child he taught himself to play piano, and after a year or so was able to perform any tune he heard by ear. I gave him violin lessons when he was nine, and he soon surpassed me on that instrument. Then he discovered the banjo, and there was no turning back. It became his passion. After moving to New York he found work with world-class orchestras. He also composed a dozen 'Hot Jazz' numbers that were published. He was barely getting started, but had accomplished so much in his twenty-five years on this earth.

The musical world lost a talent, but I lost a brother. I'd like to share some reflections on that loss with you this morning.

To Charley:
There never lived a better pal
Or brother or a friend,
And we spent the best years of our lives,
With a love that has no end.

Times Square stands like a monument,
To you since you went away,
And my happiest hours were spent with you,
In our strolls down old Broadway.

The big city doesn't seem the same,
There's memories neath those skies,

For that is where you carved your name,
In a way that never dies.

Now cheer up kid, stick to your guns,
And never mind the rain;
For someday soon I will join you,
And we'll sure be pals again."

I hear muffled crying. People leave the room. I am left alone. Later, I hear familiar footsteps. Morey lifts me and places me in my case. He zips the red velvet lining and closes the top. Secured. He carries me along.

Morey says, "Mr. Paramount, you and I are going home."

Arlington, VA: 2015

"Welcome home," the man says. He turns me around in his hands, studying me. He puts me down, gently, onto a soft chair. The room is warm, but I feel grimy. The garage's musty smell lingers. The man walks across the room, sits at a desk, and begins to make clicking sounds with his fingers. Tap, tap, tap, tap.

He returns to look at me again. Back to the desk. Tap, tap, tap. This goes on for a long time. The man mutters to himself as he taps. His 'mmm' noises remind me of the sound Charley used to make while he was composing.

Finally, he calls out. "Honey, come down here and check out what I'm doing."

A woman's voice, "I'll be there in a minute, Chuck."

He shows me to her, "You remember the banjo Dad left me. I just brought it in from the garage."

She picks me up gingerly and studies me. "Sure, I remember, but I had forgotten how beautiful it is. You should keep it in your office."

Chuck says, "Good idea. I just wrote something up. I may send it into the Post for their Sunday Magazine 'Mine' column. You know the one where you write about something you treasure. And they show a picture of it above the text. Tell me what you think."

She reads it aloud:

In the 1920's, Uncle Charley, a young musician whose name I would inherit, moved from Syracuse to Manhattan seeking work as a banjo player. He landed a job with the Paul Whiteman Orchestra, but soon found that his old Iucci was not producing the sound he wanted. He traded it, plus some cash, for a nearly new Paramount Leader Special.

It was a beauty. When he first saw it he must have thought it had come from a museum. Gold plating surrounds the drum, and there is mother of pearl inlaid work along the neck. On the back the highly polished dark wood gleams. It is set off by two thin bands of lighter wood that run around the drum and up the neck. A single line of the lighter wood bisects the drum. A touch of drama. It's a heavy instrument with a big sound, crafted for a professional musician.

Charley would play and compose on it for the rest of his career, one that included positions with Carl Fenton's Brunswick Records and Paul Whiteman's Romance of Rhythm Orchestras as well as several hot jazz compositions published by Alfred and Company. After his tragic death at twenty-five, the Paramount became my father's. And now it is mine. It needs restringing and cleaning, yet it evokes imagined stories of a young musician's life when countless couples danced to melodies played on a four string banjo.

"Not bad," the woman says. "I just have a few suggestions…"

And I have a few of my own, I think. For starters replace my A and my G string and clean my drum. Charley would never have neglected me like this. Tune me up. Then take me out and play me. I am meant to be heard.

Author's Note: Fact and Fiction

"Mr. Chen's Sweet and Sour" is based on events that occurred, but it is not an entirely factual depiction of them. Most of the characters are real, and many events I have included happened in the places, times and manner I describe. I created others to fill in gaps in the known story and to provide the reader with Morey and Charley's story as I understood it.

Morey, Charley, Frances, Joe and all the musicians in the narrative were living in either Syracuse or Manhattan in the 1920's. However, Mr. and Mrs. Chen, William and Susan Chen, Lottie Deutsch, her parents, and Tova are fictional characters as are Yetta and her cousin David. And, by extension the scenes depicted that involved the book's fictional characters did not occur.

Some events (the midnight raid depicted in Chapter 3) did occur, but Morey was not an observer. Charley and Morey did attend the Gershwin concert described in Chapter 2, and Charley's assessment of the performance is accurate. However, while Charley and Grofe were acquaintances, the conversation depicted at the concert's end did not occur. While Rabbi Friedman was a progressive leader in Syracuse's Jewish community, he did not deliver the sermon in Chapter 5.

Similarly, some of the documents included in the text were real, others were created. For example, Charley never wrote the letter to Morey in Chapter 18, but Morey did write the poem to Charley included in Chapter 28.

The primary source for the factual side of the story was 'The Life of Charles Saul Harris' by Maurice Vann Harris, my late father. I obtained this unpublished and undated manuscript after my mother's death. Some eighty typed pages in length, it was a detailed chronicle of Charley's musical career from his childhood to his passing. It contained photographs, concert programs, and sheet music some of which I have included here.

Unfortunately, my father never mentioned the document to either my brother David or to me. However as I read through the manuscript, I became intrigued. It soon became apparent that this musical biography was not merely a straightforward chronicling of a younger sibling's musical career, but a story of a love and devotion between two brothers.

Thus, the idea for this writing was born.

Chuck Harris
Arlington, VA 2017

Charley and Morey as Boys

Morey, Frances and Charley

Moonlight Serenaders

Hickville Hottentots

Cover of Rhapsodona

Charley with his Paramount Banjo

Acknowledgements

Many people have aided me in my journey from sociologist to novelist. Instructors Jerry Haines and Garrett Phelan and my fellow students in their Arlington County writing classes have provided invaluable guidance. Alan Sukoenig's knowledge of New York City's geography and musical history has been vital, as were Hillary Rubin's candid comments and ear for dialogue. Lois Stover played Rhapsodona and brought my uncle's music to life.

My brother, David Harris, and cousin, Barbara Grossman, helped fill in gaps in our family's story.

Above all, Sandy Harris, my wife and muse, provided continuing encouragement and advice, posing thoughtful questions and offering savvy suggestions from my initial scribblings to the final draft.

About the Author

Chuck Harris was born and raised in Syracuse, New York. After receiving a Ph.D. from Duke University, he and his wife moved to Northern Virginia. They currently live in Arlington.

Chuck is the father of two and the grandfather of five boys. This is his first novel.

CPSIA information can be obtained
at www.ICGtesting.com
Printed in the USA
BVOW04s0905210417
481888BV00008B/10/P